THE FURTHER ADVENTURES OF ZORRO

ADVENTURES OF ZORRO
BOOK 2

JOHNSTON MCCULLEY

PART ONE

PART I

ONE
LAND RATS AND WATER RATS

THROUGHOUT A LONG SUMMER day of more than a hundred years ago the high fog had obscured the flaming ball of sun, and the coast of Southern California had been bathed in a haze.

Then came the night, with indication of a drizzle that did not materialize. For the bank of fog suddenly was split as though with a sword, and the brilliant moon poured down, and the riven mist floated away to let the land be blessed with brilliance and the tossing sea dance in the silvery moonbeams.

Approaching the shore came a sinister vessel, craft of ill omen. She sailed slowly under a spare spread of canvas, as though fearing to reach her destination too soon, and her lights were not burning. The hiss of the waters from her bows was a lazy sort of hiss, but the more suggestive because of that. It was the playful hiss of a serpent always ready to become enraged. Her appearance betokened stealth and crime.

She was low, rakish, swift. No proper seaman commanded her, since her decks were foul and her sides badly in need of protecting paint. But her sailing gear was in perfect condition, and the man at her helm could have told that she answered to her rudder like a love-sick maiden to her swain.

Amidships stood her commander, one Barbados, a monstrous giant of a man with repugnant visage. Gigantic brass rings were in his mutilated ears. His eyes were pig-like—tiny, glittering, wholly evil. His great gnarled hands continually were forming themselves into brutish fists. He wore no shirt, no shoes. His chest and back were covered with thick, black, matted hair.

"By the saints!" he swore in a voice that drowned the slush of the waters against the vessel's sides. "Sanchez! Fools and devils! Is it necessary to shout to the world our villainy? Look at that flag flapping against the mast! Three hours after set of sun, and the flag of the devil still flies! Discipline! Ha!"

"The flag!" Sanchez bellowed. There was no definite order given, but the man nearest the mast was quick to lower the flag. Sanchez looked back toward Barbados, and Barbados grunted and turned away to look toward the distant land.

Sanchez was a smaller edition of Barbados, the evil lieutenant of an evil chief. He was short and thick, and many a man had misjudged the strength of his shoulders and arms and had discovered his sorry error too late. The eyes of Sanchez glittered also, first as he looked at Barbados, and then turned, as the chief had, to glance toward the distant land.

A fair land it was, bathed in the mellow light of the moon. Along the shore uncertain shadows played, like shapeless fairies at a game. And here was a darker streak, where a cañon ran down to the sea—a cañon with black depths caused by the rank undergrowth and stubby trees.

"There!" Barbados bellowed. He pointed toward the mouth of the cañon, where the water hissed white against a jumble of rocks. "We go ashore there, against the cliffs!"

Again there was no regular command, but the course of the pirate craft was changed a little, and she sailed slowly toward the spot Barbados had indicated. The chief grunted once more, and Sanchez hurried quickly to his side.

"We land twoscore men!" Barbados commanded. "Twoscore will be enough. I lead them, and you are to go with me. The others will remain aboard and take the ship off shore again, and return to-morrow night two hours before the dawn."

"*Sí!*" Sanchez said.

"'Tis to be a pretty party, by the saints! Rich loot, food and wines, honey and olives, gold and jewels and precious stones! Bronze native wenches for such as like them! And time enough for it, eh? Ha! For some four months we have sailed up and down the coast, now and then landing and raiding to get a few pigs and cows. 'Tis time for a bold stroke! And this—"

"It is arranged?" Sanchez questioned.

"Am I in the habit of rushing in where things are not arranged?" Barbados demanded. "Señor Pirate, do you take me to be a weak and silly fool?"

"If I did," Sanchez replied, "I would have more wit than to say so to your face!"

"Ha! Is it arranged? When the Governor's own man arranges it? There is a precious pair, the Governor and his man!" said Barbados, laughing raucously. "Pirates and rogues we may be, but we can take lessons in villainy from some of the gentry who bear the names of *caballeros,* but have foul blood in their veins!"

"The thing has an evil look," Sanchez was bold enough to assert. "I like not a task too easy. By my naked blade, that which looks easy often is not! If this should prove to be a trap—"

Barbados gave a cry of rage and whirled toward him suddenly, and Sanchez retreated a single step, and his hand dropped to the naked cutlass in his belt of tanned human skin.

"Try to draw it, fool!" Barbados cried. "I'll have you choked black in the face and hurled overboard for shark meat before your hand reaches the blade!"

"I made no move to draw," Sanchez wailed.

"There are times when I wonder why I allow you to remain at my side," Barbados told him, folding his gigantic arms across his hairy chest. "And there are times when I wonder whether your heart is not turning to that of a woman and your blood to water or swill. A trap, you fool! Am I the man to walk into traps? Kindly allow me to attend to the finer details of this business. And a pretty business it is!"

"The village of Reina de Los Angeles is miles in the interior," Sanchez wailed. "I do not like to get out of sight of the sea. With the pitching planks of a deck beneath my bare feet—"

"Beware lest you have beneath your feet the plank that is walked until a man reaches its end and drops to watery death!" Barbados warned him. "Enough of this! Pick the men who are to land, and get ready the boats!"

An hour later the anchor had been dropped, and the pirate craft had swung with the tide and was tugging at her chains like a puppy at a leash. Over the sides went the boats, Barbados growling soft curses at the noise his men made.

"We have nothing to fear, fools and devils!" he said. "But there will be no surprise if some converted native sees us and carries to Reina de Los Angeles word of our arrival. There is many a *hacienda* in these parts where pirates are detested. Silence, rogues! You'll have your fill of noise to-morrow night!"

Without knowing it, Barbados practiced a deal of psychology. These wild men of the sea had before them a journey of some miles inland, and they knew it and hated it, but the pirate chief continually hinted to them of the rich loot at the end of the present trip, and his hints served their purpose well.

Toward the shore they rowed, tossing on the breakers, making for the dark spot where the cañon ran down into the sea. There a cliff some twelve feet high circled back into the land, forming a natural shelter against the land breeze at times and the sea winds at other times.

Through the surf they splashed, half naked, carrying naught except their weapons, and no weapons save their cutlasses. They gathered on the beach and watched the boats return to the ship, shrieking coarse jests at the men compelled to remain behind.

Barbados took from his belt a tiny scrap of parchment and looked at it closely. With him this passed for a map. He called Sanchez to his side, turned his back to the sea, and looked along the dark reaches of the cañon.

"Forward!" Barbados said. "And let there be little noise about it! If we stumble across one of the accursed natives, slit his throat and so silence it."

"And if we meet a wandering *fray* of the missions, slit him into ribbons," Sanchez added, chuckling.

To his wonder, Barbados grasped his arm so that Sanchez thought the bone must break.

"Enough of that!" Barbados cried. "Touch no *fray* in violence except I give the word!"

"You love the robes and gowns?" Sanchez asked, in wonder.

"I love to protect myself," Barbados replied. "It is an ill thing to assault a *fray* if it can be avoided." He stopped speaking for a moment, and seemed to shiver throughout the length and breadth of his gigantic frame. "I had a friend once who struck a *fray*," he added in a whisper. "I do not like to remember what happened to him. Forward!"

Inland they tramped, mile after mile, keeping to the cañons, following an *arroyo* now and then, dodging from dark spot to dark spot, while Barbados growled curses at the bright moon and Sanchez continually admonished the men behind to keep silent.

It was a journey they disliked, but they liked to think of the loot they would find at the end of it. On they went, toward the sleeping town of Reina de Los Angeles. Besides Barbados and Sanchez, few of them had seen the town. Pirates had been treated harshly there when they had wandered inland. But now something had happened, it appeared, that made a raid on the town a comparatively safe enterprise.

An hour before dawn they stumbled across a native, caught him as he started to flee, and left his lifeless body behind. Then came the day, and they went into hiding in a jumble of hills, within easy striking distance of the town. They had covered ground well.

Sprawled on the sward they slept. Barbados, a little way aside, consulted his poor map once more, and then called Sanchez to his side.

"Since we may have to split our force, it were well that you knew more of this business," he said.

"I am listening, Barbados."

"This man who is to meet us to-morrow night at the edge of the town is a high official."

"I have heard you call him the Governor's man."

"Even so. He is to have matters arranged so that the town will be at our mercy. It never has been raided properly. It will be necessary, perhaps, to steal horses, and possibly a *carreta* or two in which to carry the loot. The town will be wide open for us, my friend."

"There is a *presidio* in Reina de Los Angeles, and where there is a *presidio* there are soldiers," Sanchez reminded him.

"And where there are soldiers there are fools," Barbados added. He stopped speaking long enough to chuckle. "I am not afraid of the soldiers. This man with whom we are to deal will care for the troops."

"I fail to understand it," Sanchez said, shaking his head. "Why should such things be? Do we split the loot with this high official?"

"Dream of innocence, listen!" Barbados hissed. "Listen, and comprehend, else I choke you to death! An emissary came to me in the south from this high official, and through him arrangements were made. Things have happened since last we were in the vicinity of Reina de Los Angeles. The Governor, I know, left San Francisco de Asis and journeyed south with his gallant company. And while he was at Reina de Los Angeles something happened that caused him to hate the town. There even was talk for a time of him being forced to abdicate his high station."

"Ha! More mystery!" Sanchez growled.

"It seems that in the southland there was a pest of a highwayman known as Señor Zorro, and whom men called the Curse of Capistrano. A land pirate, spit upon him! How can a man be a pirate on the land? However, this Señor Zorro did several things worthy of note. From what I have heard, I would we had a dozen of him in the ship's company. We could raid the whole of Mexico, capture the Spanish fleets and attack Europe."

"This Señor Zorro must be quite some man," Sanchez observed.

"I have heard but little, but enough to convince me that I would have him for a friend rather than an enemy. He is a sort of devil. Now he is here and now he is gone. Like a ghost he comes and like a specter he disappears. Ha! You, a pirate, cross yourself!"

"I am afraid of no live man who lives, save perhaps yourself," Sanchez observed. "But I like not this talk of ghosts."

"Here is the jest, fool and friend! It develops after a time that this terrible Señor Zorro is nothing but a *caballero* out to have a bit of fun and protect the weak. There is a waste of time for you—protecting the weak. And other sundry *caballeros* joined hands with him and punished minor officials who sought to steal and deal crookedly. That is right and proper. If a thief, be a thief! If a pirate, be a pirate! But do not play at being an honest man and try to be thief and pirate at the same time."

"Ha!" Sanchez grunted, meaning that he wished the sermon to end and the tale to continue.

"This Señor Zorro, whose real name I have forgotten if ever I knew it, carved his initial with his sword into the cheeks and foreheads of many men. They call it the Mark of Zorro. And when his identity was disclosed his friends stood by him and told the Governor that it were best if he return to San Francisco de Asis and grace Reina de Los Angeles with his continual absence."

"And did he?"

"He did," Barbados replied, "with hatred in his heart for this same Reina de Los Angeles. He did not abdicate, of course. And he craves revenge."

"Ha! Here is where we enter?"

"It is," Barbados replied. "We raid the town and take what we will, and the Governor hears of it, sends soldiers running wildly up and down the coast, and winks at himself in his looking-glass. For the information and protection we get, we hand to the Governor's man at a certain time and place a certain share of the loot. Which we well can afford, since we are to get it so easily."

"If we forget to hand it—" Sanchez began.

"Friend and fool! By the saints! Are you an honest pirate or no? We shall deal fairly. Think of the future. It is not only Reina de Los Angeles. There is San Juan Capistrano, and rich San Diego de Alcála to come after. By that time we have this pretty Governor and certain of his officials in our mesh, and do as we will. Ha! What knaves! I would rather be an honest pirate than a politician any day!"

The day passed and the dusk came. And once yet again Barbados indulged in curses. For it was a beautiful moonlight night, half as light as the day that had just died, and a man could be seen afar. But Barbados led his wretched company on toward the town, and after a time they came to the crest of a slope and saw lights twinkling in the distance.

Stretched on the ground so as not to form a silhouette against the sky, Barbados looked over the scene. He could see the plaza, fires burning before the huts of the natives, twinkling lights in the windows of the pretentious houses where lived the men of wealth and blood and rank. To one side was the *presidio*, and to the other the church.

Barbados grunted an order to Sanchez and crept forward alone. He approached the end of the village, reached a spot where the shadows were deep, and crouched to wait.

For half an hour he waited, grumbling his impatience. Then there came to him a figure muffled in a long cloak. Barbados hissed a word that had been agreed upon. The figure stepped quickly to his side.

"You are ready?"

"Ready, *señor*," Barbados replied.

"Where are your men?"

"In hiding three hundred yards away, *señor*."

"It were best to strike in about an hour. The soldiers will be sent toward the south on a wild goose chase."

"I understand, *señor*."

"I ride back toward the hills to a *hacienda* to pay a social call. It would not do for me to be here, of course."

"Certainly not, *señor*."

"The way will be open to you. Take your will with the town, but do not use the torch, except it be on the hut of some native. As soon as you have your loot, make for the sea again. The soldiers will be sent on a useless trail."

"It is well arranged, *señor*. We'll strike as soon as the troopers are at a sufficient distance."

"There is something else. You must send a few men of your force to the *hacienda* of Don Carlos Pulido, three miles to the north."

"What is this, *señor*?" Barbados asked.

"A little matter of abducting a woman for me."

"Ha!"

"The Señorita Lolita Pulido, understand. She is to be seized and conducted to the coast and taken aboard ship. She is not to be harmed, but treated with every respect. In four or five days I shall meet you at the rendezvous on the southern coast, and claim her as my share of the loot. Do this well, and that is all the share of loot I ask this time."

"A mere detail," Barbados said.

"If the *hacienda* is disturbed a bit during the abduction, it will not cause the heartbreak of the Governor. This Don Carlos Pulido is no friend of His Excellency."

"I understand, *señor*."

"The *señorita* expects to become the bride to-morrow of Don Diego Vega—curse him! That large house at the side of the plaza is his. When you are raiding the town, Barbados, pay special attention to that house. And should he get a knife between his ribs there will be no sorrow on my part."

"I begin to comprehend," Barbados replied.

"I may depend upon you?"

"*Sí, señor*! We attend to the house of this Don Diego Vega and to the don personally. I shall send a small force to abduct the girl and take her to the shore. She will be waiting for you at the rendezvous to the south."

"Good! Watch when the soldiers ride away, and strike an hour later. *Adios!*"

The cloak dropped for a moment as the man from the village straightened himself. Barbados got a good look at his face as the moonlight struck it. He gasped.

"Your forehead!" he said.

"It is nothing. That cursed beast of a Zorro put it there!"

Barbados looked again. On the man's forehead was a ragged "Z," put there in such a manner that it would remain forever. There was a moment of silence, and then Barbados found himself alone. The other had slipped away through the shadows.

Barbados grinned. "Here is a double deal of some sort, but it need bring me no fear," he mused. "Here would be startling news for all men to know. Wants to steal a girl now, does he? For his share of proper loot I'd steal him half a score of girls!"

He grinned again and started back toward his men. Barbados did not fear the soldiers, and he knew they would be sent away. He could be sure of that. For the conspirator who had come to him out of the dark was none other than Captain Ramón, *commandante* of the *presidio* at Reina de Los Angeles.

TWO
PEDRO THE BOASTER

SERGEANT PEDRO GONZALES, a giant of a wine-guzzling soldier whose heart was as large as his capacity for liquor, was known as "Pedro the Boaster." When there were military duties to be done he was to be found at his post in the *presidio,* but at other times one found him at the village *posada,* sitting before the big fireplace and remaking the world with words.

On this moonlight night, Sergeant Pedro Gonzales crossed the plaza with a corporal and a couple of soldiers, entered the inn, and called in a loud voice for the landlord to fetch wine and be quick about it. The sergeant had learned long since that the fat landlord held him in terror, and did he but act surly and displeased he received excellent service.

"Landlord, you are as fat as your wine is thin!" Sergeant Pedro declared, sprawling at one of the tables. "I have a suspicion now and then that you keep a special wineskin for me, and mix water with my drink."

"*Señor!*" the landlord protested.

"We honest soldiers are stationed here to protect you from liars and thieves and dishonest travelers up and down El Camino Real, and you treat us like the dirt beneath your boots."

"*Señor!* I have the greatest respect—"

"One of these fine days," Gonzales interrupted, "there will be trouble. Some gentleman of the highway will approach you with an idea of robbery, and you'll shriek for the soldiery. And then, fat one, I may remember the watered wine, and be busy elsewhere!"

"But I protest—" the landlord began.

"More wine!" the sergeant shouted. "Must I get out my blade and carve your wineskins—or your own skin? More wine of the best, and you'll get your pay when I get mine, if it is an honest score you keep. If my friend, Don Diego Vega, was here—!"

"That same friend of yours makes merry a little later in the evening," the landlord said, as he went to fill the wine cups. "To-morrow he is to take a bride."

"Pig, do you suppose I do not know it?" Gonzales screeched. "Think you that I have been asleep these past few months? Was I not in the thick of it when Don Diego Vega played at being Señor Zorro?"

"You were in the thick of it," the corporal admitted, with a touch of sarcasm in his voice.

"Ha!" cried the sergeant. "There was a turbulent time for you! Here in this very room I fought him, blade to blade, thinking that he was some stinking highwayman. And just as I was getting the better of it—"

"How is this?" the corporal shrieked.

"Just as I was getting the better of the blade match," Gonzales reaffirmed, glaring at the corporal, "back he went and dashed through the door! And thereafter he set the town about its own ears for some time to come."

"It occurs to me that I saw that fight," the corporal declared. "If you were getting the best of it at any stage, then were mine eyes at fault."

"I know a man," said the sergeant, darkly, "who will do extra guard duty for a score of days."

"Ha!" the corporal grunted. "You do not like plain speech!"

"I do not like a soldier to make mock of his superiors," the sergeant replied. "It were unseemly for me to make remarks, for instance, concerning our *commandante,* Captain Ramón, but let it be said that he fought this Señor Zorro, too. And Captain Ramón wears on his forehead Zorro's mark. You will notice that there is no carved Z on my face!"

"Ha!" the corporal grunted again. "It were best, sergeant, to voice such remarks inwardly. The *commandante* is not proud of the mark he wears."

Gonzales changed the subject. "The wine!" he thundered. "It goes well on a moonlight night, the same as on a stormy one. But moonlight is a poor business save for lovesick swains. 'Tis no night for a soldier. Would one expect thieves to descend through the moonlight?"

"There be pirates," the corporal said.

"Pirates!" Gonzales's great fist descended and met the table with a crash, sending the wine cups bouncing. "Pirates! You have noticed no pirates in Reina de Los Angeles, have you? They have not been playing around the *presidio,* have they? I am not saying that they know I am stationed here, however—Meal mush and goat's milk! Pirates is my dish!"

"The town grows wealthy, and they may come," the corporal said.

"You fear? You tremble?" Gonzales cried. "Are you soldier or *fray*? Pirates! By the saints, I would that they came! My sword arm grows fat from little use."

"Talk not of pirates!" the landlord begged. "Suppose they did come?"

"And what if they did?" Gonzales demanded. "Am I not here, dolt? Are there not soldiers? Pirates? Ha!"

He sprang to his feet, those same feet spread wide apart. His hand darted down, and he whipped out his blade.

"That for a pirate!" he shouted, and made a mighty thrust at the wall. "This for a pirate!" And he slashed through the air, his blade whistling so that the corporal and soldiers sprang backward, and the four or five natives who happened to be in the inn cringed in a corner. "Pirates!" cried Gonzales. "I would I could meet one this very night! We grew stale from inaction. There is too much peace in the world! Meal mush and goat's milk!"

The door opened suddenly. Sergeant Gonzales stopped in the middle of a sentence, and his blade stopped in the middle of an arc. And then the sergeant and the other soldiers snapped to attention, for the *commandante* was before them.

"Sergeant Gonzales!" Captain Ramón commanded.

"*Sí!*"

"I could hear you shouting half way across the plaza. If you wish to meet a pirate, perhaps you may have your wish. Rumors have been brought by natives. Mount your men and proceed along El Camino Real toward the south. Search the country well, once you are four or five miles from the town. It is a bright moonlight night, and men may be seen at a great distance."

"It is an order!" the sergeant admitted.

"Leave but one man at the *presidio* as guard. Return before dawn. Have my best horse made ready, as I ride out to a *hacienda* for a visit. Go!"

"*Sí!*" Sergeant Gonzales grunted. He motioned to the soldiers, and they hurried through the door. He sheathed his sword, and when the back of Captain Ramón was turned for an instant he tossed off the wine that had been before him, and hurried after his men. The *commandante* drew off his gloves and sat at one of the tables.

Gonzales led the way across the plaza and toward the *presidio*. He was growling low down in his throat.

"This is a fine state of affairs!" he said. "Ride all night and kick up the dust! Back before dawn with nothing done!"

"But you wanted pirates," the corporal protested.

"Think you they will stand in the middle of El Camino Real and await our pleasure?" Gonzales growled. "What pirate would be abroad a night like this? Could we but meet some—ha! There is a special reward for pirates!"

Even before they had reached the entrance of the *presidio,* he began shouting his orders. Torches flared, and men ran to prepare the horses. Fifteen minutes later, with Gonzales at their head, they rode across the plaza and out upon El Camino Real, their mounts snorting, their sabers rattling.

From the crest of a slope a few hundred yards away, Barbados and his evil crew watched them depart upon their mounts.

THREE
SUDDEN TURMOIL

WHILE THE BLUSHES played across her cheeks, Señorita Lolita Pulido sat at one end of the big table in the great living-room of her father's house and watched the final preparations for her wedding.

Don Carlos, her gray-haired father, watched proudly from the foot of the table. Doña Catalina, her mother, walked majestically around the room and gave soft commands. Native servants scurried like rats in and out of the great room, carrying bundles of silks and satins, gowns, intimate garments.

"To-morrow!" Don Carlos sighed, and in the sigh was that which spoke of cruelties bravely borne. "To-morrow, *señorita*, you become the bride of Don Diego Vega, and the first lady of Reina de Los Angeles. And my troubles, let us hope, are at an end."

"Let us hope so," said Doña Catalina.

"The Governor himself dare not raise his hand against the father-in-law of Don Diego Vega. My fortunes will increase again. And you, daughter of my heart, will be a great lady, with wealth at your command."

"And love also," the little *señorita* said, bowing her head.

"Love, also!" said Doña Catalina.

"Ha!" Don Carlos cried, with a gale of laughter. "It is love now, is it? And when first Don Diego came wooing, the girl would have none of him, even to better the family fortunes. He was dull, he yawned, and she wanted a man of hot blood and romantic. But when it was learned that he was Señor Zorro—That made a difference! Love, also! It is well!"

Señorita Lolita blushed again, and fumbled at a soft garment upon her lap.

There came a pounding at the door, and one of the servants opened it. Don Carlos glanced up to find a man of the village there.

"It is a message, *señor*," he said.

"From whom?" Don Carlos asked.

"From Don Diego Vega, to the little *señorita*."

Señorita Lolita dimpled, and her black eyes flashed as she bent over the heap of garments again. Don Carlos stood up and stalked majestically toward the door.

"I take the message," he said, and he took it, and handed it to Doña Catalina, that she might read it first. "Don Diego Vega is not wed to my daughter as yet. It is not proper that he send her sealed messages."

His eyes were twinkling as he turned away. Señorita Lolita pouted and pretended indifference, and Doña Catalina, her mother, unfolded the message, and read it with a smile upon her lips.

"It is harmless," she announced.

Señorita Lolita looked up, and took the message from her mother's hand. Don Diego Vega, it appeared, wasted no words. His message was read swiftly:

This man has orders to make a record carrying this greeting of love to you and fetching yours in return.

Thine,

DIEGO.

"Ha!" Don Carlos shouted. "Economy is a great thing, but not in words when there is love to be spoken. You should have seen the messages I sent to Catalina in the old days!"

"Carlos!" Doña Catalina warned.

"And paid a native wench royally to slip them to her," Don Carlos continued, shamelessly. "Behind the back of her *duenna*! Page after page, and every word a labor! I could fight better than I could write!"

"Perhaps so can Don Diego," the little *señorita* said.

"Staunch and loyal to him, are you?" Don Carlos roared. "That is proper. Pen your reply, my daughter, and let this man establish his record for the return trip to Reina de Los Angeles. Do not keep Don Diego waiting."

The *señorita* blushed yet again, got up, and swept into a room adjoining.

Don Carlos addressed the messenger: "How are things in the town?"

"Don Diego entertains his *caballero* friends at a last bachelor supper, *señor*," the man replied.

"Ha! Young men only, I suppose?"

"Sí, señor!"

"Wine flows, I take it, and the table is piled high with rich food?"

"Sí, señor!"

"Ah, well! I shall have my turn to-morrow at the marriage feast," Don Carlos said. "My regards to Don Diego Vega!"

"They shall be given him, *señor*."

The *señorita* returned and handed what she had written to her mother, who perused it and sealed it, and handed it to the messenger in turn. The man bobbed his head in respectful salute, and hurried out. A native servant closed the door behind him—but neglected to drop the heavy bar in place. Because of the unusual excitement, none noticed.

Don Carlos resumed his position at the foot of the table. This was a great night for him, and to-morrow would be a great day. He was happy because his fortunes were on the mend, because the Governor had been forced to cease his persecutions. But he was happy also because his daughter was to have happiness.

Don Carlos and his wife had lavished upon this, their only child, love enough for a dozen. And now both glanced at her as she fumbled at a silken shawl. Her black eyes were sparkling again, though dreams were glistening in them. Her cheeks were delicately flushed. Her dainty hands played with the silks. One tiny tip of a boot peeped from beneath her voluminous skirts. A bride of whom any man could honestly be proud, Don Carlos thought, and with proper blood in her veins and proper thoughts in her head.

"So Don Diego makes merry to-night with his young friends!" Don Carlos said. "I would like to peer in upon him now."

Could he have done so, he would have seen a merry gathering. In the big living-room of Don Diego's town *casa* a huge table had been spread. Don Diego sat at the head of it, dressed in fastidious garments, and *caballeros* were grouped around it. Richly dressed they were, with blades at their sides, blades with jeweled hilts, but serviceable weapons for all that. Wine cups and dishes were before them. They feasted, and they drank. They toasted Don Diego, and the Señorita Lolita, Don Diego's father, and the *señorita's* father, and one another.

"Another good man gone wrong!" cried Don Audre Ruiz. He sat at Don Diego's right hand, because he was Don Diego's closest friend. "Here is our comrade, Don Diego, about to turn into a family man!" he continued. "This scion of Old Spain, this delicate morsel of *caballero* blood to be gobbled up by the monster of matrimony! It is time to weep!"

"Into your wine cup!" Don Diego added.

"Ha!" Don Audre Ruiz cried. "But a few days ago, it seems, we rode after him as though he had been the devil, rode hard upon his heels, thinking that we were following some sort of renegade *caballero* playing at highwayman. Señor Zorro, by the saints! We shouted praises of him because for a time he took us out of our monotony. Then came the unmasking, and we found that Don Diego and Señor Zorro were one and the same!"

He ceased speaking long enough to empty his wine cup and make certain that a servant refilled it.

"Señor Zorro!" he continued. "Those were happy moments! And now he is to turn husband, and no more riding abroad with sword in hand. We shall die of monotony, Diego, my friend!"

"Of fat!" Don Diego corrected.

"What has become of the wild blood that coursed your veins for a few moons?" Don Audre Ruiz demanded. "Where are those precious, turbulent drops that were in Zorro?"

"They linger," Don Diego declared. "It needs but the cause to churn them into active being."

"Ha! A cause! *Caballeros*, let us find him a cause, that this good friend of ours will be too busy to get married."

"One moment!" Don Diego cried. He stood up and smiled at them, gave a little twitch to his shoulders, and then turned his back upon the brilliant company and hurried from the room. They drank again, and waited. And after a time, back he came, a silk-draped bundle beneath one arm.

"What mystery is this?" Don Audre demanded. He sprawled back in his chair and prepared to laugh. It was said of Don Audre that he always was prepared to laugh. He laughed when he made love, when he fought, as he ate and drank, his bubbling spirit, always upon his lips.

"Here is no mystery," Don Diego Vega declared. He smiled at them again, unwrapped what he held, and suddenly exhibited a sword. "The blade of Zorro!" he cried.

There was an instant of silence, and then every *caballero* sprang to his feet. Their own swords came flashing from their scabbards, flashed on high, reflected in a million rays the glowing lights of the candelabra.

"Zorro!" they shouted. "Zorro!"

"Good old blade!" Don Diego said, a whimsical smile playing about his lips.

"Good old point!" exclaimed Don Audre Ruiz. "With it you marked many a scoundrel with your mark, notably and especially one Captain Ramón. Why do we endure his presence here in Reina de Los Angeles? Why not force the Governor to send him north?"

"Let us not mar a perfect evening with thoughts of him," Don Diego begged. "*Caballeros*, I have brought this blade before you for a purpose. We have drunk toasts to everything of which we could think, and there still remains an abundance of rare wine that has not been guzzled. A toast to the sword of Zorro!"

"Ha! A happy thought!" Don Audre Ruiz cried. "*Caballeros*, a toast to the sword of Zorro!"

They drank it, put down their golden goblets, and sighed. They glanced at one another, each thinking of the days when Señor Zorro had ruled El Camino Real for a time. And then they dropped into their chairs once more, and Don Diego Vega sat down also, the sword on the table before him.

"It was a great game," he said, and sighed himself. "But it is in the past. Now I shall be a man of peace and quiet."

"That remains to be seen," Don Audre declared. "There may be domestic warfare, you know. A man takes a terrible chance when he weds."

"Nothing but peace and quiet," Don Diego responded. "The sword of Zorro is but a relic. Years from now I may look upon it and smile. It has served its purpose."

He yawned.

"By the saints!" Don Audre Ruiz breathed. "Did you see him? He yawned! While yet the word 'Zorro' was upon his lips, he yawned. And this is the man who defended persecuted priests and natives, defied the soldiery and made the Governor do a dance! 'Tis a cause he wants and needs, something to change him into Zorro again!"

"To-morrow I become a husband," Don Diego answered him, yawning yet once more and fumbling with a handkerchief. "By the way, *señores*, have you ever seen this one?"

He spread the handkerchief over the wine goblet before him, and as the *caballeros* bent forward to watch, smiles upon their faces, he passed one hand rapidly back and forth across the covered goblet with such rapidity that it was hidden almost all the time, and with the other hand he reached beneath the edge of the handkerchief and jerked the goblet away, letting it drop to the floor. The handkerchief collapsed on the table. Don Diego waved a hand languidly.

"See? It is gone!" he breathed.

"Bah!" Don Audre cried as the others laughed. "At your boy's tricks again, are you? Where is your wild blood now?"

"I am done with roistering and adventure."

"A man never knows when his words may be hurled back at him and cause him to look foolish," said Don Audre. "It is foolish to take everything for granted. For instance—"

He stopped. The sounds of a tumult had reached their ears. For a moment they were silent, listening. Shouts, oaths, the sounds of blows, the clashing of blades.

"What in the name of the saints is that?" Don Diego asked.

A trembling servant answered him.

"There are men fighting over by the inn, *señor,*" he said. "I heard some one shout of pirates!"

FOUR
FRAY FELIPE MAKES A VOW

BARBADOS CONTINUED to mutter curses as he watched the sky. Not a cloud marred its face, and the moon was at the full. But here was an enterprise where there was small risk, so he could discount the bright night.

He grunted his pleasure as he saw Sergeant Gonzales and the troopers ride away from the *presidio*, cross the plaza, and continue toward the south. He called Sanchez to him and explained what was to be done at the *hacienda* of Don Carlos Pulido.

"You will take half a dozen men," Barbados commanded. "Do as you please at the place, but capture the *señorita* by all means, and go quickly back over the hills to the mouth of the cañon. Steal horses, and ride. Get there before the break of day! We shall do the same. The ship will be putting in at dawn or before."

"*Sí!*" Sanchez replied. "And do you care for my share of the loot here. There may be small profit at the *hacienda*!"

Sanchez selected his ruffians and led them away around a hill and toward the north, where the *hacienda* of Don Carlos Pulido rested. Barbados whispered instructions to the remainder of the crew. And then they waited, for Barbados wished to make sure that the soldiers did not return.

For more than an hour longer he waited, and then gave the word. Down from the crest of the slope they slipped, breathing heavily, lusting for illegal gain, holding their cutlasses in readiness for instant use. They kept in the scant shadows as much as possible, scattered as they crossed the wider light spaces, made their way slowly to the edge of the town.

There, in the shadows cast by an empty adobe building, they separated, and Barbados whispered his final instructions. They were to look for rich loot, and nothing bulky. He had decided against food and wine, bolts of cloth, casks of olives and jars of honey. Such things could be obtained later at any *hacienda*. Just now he wished to get portable valuables and hurry back to the coast.

Men were detailed to seize horses and have them in readiness. Certain large houses were to be attacked in force after the smaller ones had been disposed of. The inn was to receive special attention, since it was whispered that the fat landlord had hidden wealth.

Down upon the town they crept, and suddenly they charged into the plaza from either side. Into the inn they poured, cutting and slashing at natives until they fled screeching with terror, stabbing at the fat landlord as he called upon the saints.

They took what the landlord had, and gave their attention to the houses and shops. And now bedlam broke loose as it was realized what was taking place. Doors were smashed, terrified men and women were driven from room to room. Things of value were seized. Jewels were ripped from dainty throats and delicate fingers. Silken shawls were torn from beautiful shoulders.

Here and there a man gave fight, but not for long. The pirates outnumbered the citizens, because they traveled in force and the citizens were scattered. Shrieks and screeches and cries stabbed the air. Raucous oaths and fiendish laughter rang across the plaza. And above the din roared the voice of Barbados, the human fiend, as he ordered his men, commanded them, admonished them, led them to an easy victory.

It was quick work, because the descent had been so unexpected. It might have continued throughout the night, until the town was stripped bare, until not a native's hut was left standing. But Barbados wanted quick loot and a getaway. He wanted to reach the coast during the bright moonlight, get the planks of the ship's deck beneath his feet once more. He trusted Captain Ramón, but he feared that the soldiers might return.

Across the plaza the pirates charged, with Barbados at their head. They broke into the church. They filled the sacred edifice with oaths and ribald jest and raucous laughter. They darted here and there, torches held high above their heads, searching for articles of worth.

From a little room to one side stepped a *fray*. His hair was silver, his face was calm. Erect and purposeful he stood, looking across at them. Quick steps forward he took toward the altar, where there were relics he loved.

"What do you here, *señores*?" he demanded.

His voice seemed soft, yet at the same time there was the ring of steel in it. They stopped, their shouting ceased, there was a moment of silence.

"Who are you?" one shouted.

"I am called Fray Felipe, *señores,*" came the response. "Just now I am in charge of this house of worship. How is it that you so far forget yourselves as to bring your tumult here?"

"*Fray?*" one shouted. "Fool and *fray*? Why do we bring our tumult here? For to get loot, gowned one!"

"Loot?" Fray Felipe thundered, taking another step forward. "You would profane this house? You would lay sacrilegious hands on what is to be found here, even as you have voiced sacrilegious tones within these walls? Scum of the earth, begone!"

They surged toward him. "One side, *fray*!" shouted a foremost one. "Respect the black flag and we respect your gown!"

"Spawn of hell! Sons of the devil!" Fray Felipe thundered. "Back to the door, and out of this holy place!"

He scarcely hoped to stop them. There were rich ornaments on the altar, and in the uncertain light the torches shed he could see the eyes of those nearest glittering. And the gem-studded goblet was there!

Thought of the gem-studded goblet gave new strength to ancient Fray Felipe. It was a relic highly prized. Fray Felipe loved it, and cared for it tenderly. There was a legend connected with it. Once it had been touched by a saint's lips, men had said. To have this scum as much as touch the sacred goblet was too much—to have them steal it would be unthinkable.

Once more they surged forward, and Fray Felipe sprang before the altar and threw up his hands in a gesture of command.

"Back!" he cried. "Would you damn beyond recovery your immortal souls? Would you commit the unpardonable sin?"

"Ha!" shouted a man in the front of the throng. "Worry not about our souls, *fray*! One side, else you'll have a chance to worry about the state of your own! We have scant time to spend on a *fray*!"

"What would you?" Fray Felipe asked.

"Loot, fool of a *fray*!"

"Only over my dead body do you take it! I am not afraid to die to protect holy things! But you—you will fear to die, if you do this thing!"

"Slit his throat!" cried one in the throng. "Are we here to argue? The work is not done!"

Once more they surged forward. The light of the torches sent rays of fire shooting from the ornaments on the altar. Their lust for loot consumed them.

Fray Felipe braced himself, seized the nearest, raised him half from the floor, and hurled him back against his fellows.

"The *fray* shows fight!" one cried. "Use your knives, you in the front! A stab between the ribs, and let us go!"

Again they rushed, and Fray Felipe prepared for one more feeble attempt, the one he deemed would be the last. He made the sign of the cross and waited calmly—waited until they were upon him, until he could feel their hot breathing upon his face, until the stench of their perspiration was in his nostrils.

But, even as a man raised a cutlass to strike, there came an interruption. The bellowing voice of Barbados rang out above the din.

"Stop!" he shrieked. There was something terrifying in the sudden and unexpected command. The pirates stopped, fell back. Barbados charged through them and to Fray Felipe's side. The pirate's face showed white in the light of the torches.

"Back!" he commanded. "This *fray* is not to be harmed! Out, fools and devils! There is one rich house yet to be robbed. Let us not tarry here!"

"There is loot—" one began.

He did not complete the sentence. Barbados whirled, and with a single blow he stretched him senseless.

"Out!" he commanded. "This *fray* is not to be touched!"

They backed away from him, rushed back to gather near the door. They did not pretend to understand this, but Barbados was chief, and perhaps he knew what he was doing. They saw him turn, knew that he spoke to the *fray*, but could not make out his words.

"I had no doing in this," Barbados said. "I assault no *fray* nor priest! I stopped them in time. Had I not remained outside a moment to watch affairs I would have stopped them before."

"You are not wholly bad," Fray Felipe said.

"I am wholly bad, *fray*—make no mistake about it! But I keep my hands off *frailes* and priests!"

He whirled around and rushed to the door, shrieking at his men. Only the soft light of the candles glowed in the church.

Fray Felipe took a step forward and looked after them. He turned back toward the altar, a look of thankfulness in his face.

And suddenly that look changed! Misery took its place. Fray Felipe gave a little cry of mingled surprise and pain, and tottered forward. The precious gem-studded goblet was gone!

He sensed at once how it had happened. When they had charged upon him, before Barbados came, one of the pirates had snatched the goblet away.

Fray Felipe whirled toward the door again, took half a dozen steps, seemed at the point of rushing after them. But he knew they were on the other side of the plaza now, and that an appeal to them would be useless. However, he could try.

He faced the altar again, and the expression of his old countenance was wonderful to see. And then and there Fray Felipe took a vow.

"I go!" he said. "I return with the saintly goblet, or do not return at all!"

FIVE
ZORRO TAKES THE TRAIL

BARBADOS HAD SAVED the *casa* of Don Diego Vega for the last. He had kept an eye upon it, however, while his men were looting the town, but had seen nothing to indicate danger from that quarter. And now he remembered Captain Ramón's commands, and it pleased him to carry them out.

Don Diego's was the finest house in the village, and seemed to promise rich loot. Barbados placed four of his men outside to guard against the unexpected return of the soldiers, and led the remainder straight to the front door.

They hesitated there for a moment, gathered closely together, then Barbados gave the word, and they rushed through the door and hurled themselves inside, to go sprawling over the rich rugs and carpets and stop in astonishment and confusion. Barbados swore a great oath as he strove to maintain his balance.

Before them was a wonderful room lavishly furnished. To one side was a wide stairway that led to the upper regions of the house, and priceless tapestries were hanging from a mezzanine. But what engaged the attention of Barbados and his crew the most was the big table in the middle of the room and some score of richly dressed *caballeros* sitting around it.

Here was the unexpected, which Barbados always feared. He came to a stop, thrust forward his head, and his little eyes began glittering. The soldiers were gone from the town, but here were a score of young *caballeros* who were fully as good as soldiers in a fight, and who loved fighting. Barbados had seen such young blades handle swords and rapiers before.

The entrance of the pirates had followed closely upon the announcement of their presence in the town to Don Diego by the servant. And when they tumbled through the door, showing their evil faces in the strong light, the *caballeros* struggled to get to their feet, reaching for their blades, the smiles swept from their faces and expressions of grim determination showing there instead. But the calm voice of Don Diego quieted them.

"Ha!" Don Diego said. "What have we here? *Señores,* it is the night before my wedding, and most persons are welcome to partake of my hospitality. But this happens to be a select gathering of my close friends, and I really cannot remember of having sent you invitations."

"Have done!" Barbados bellowed, his voice ringing with a courage he scarcely felt. "Have done, fashionable fop! We are men who sail under the black flag, terrible alike on land and sea!"

Don Diego Vega threw back his head and laughed lightly.

"Did you hear that, Audre, my friend?" he asked Ruiz. "This fellow says that he and his comrades are terrible alike on land and sea."

Don Audre entered into the spirit of the occasion, as he always did. "Diego, I did not know that you were such a wit," he said. "Have you hired these fellows to come here and give us a fright? Ha! It is a merry jest, one that I'll remember to my last day! For a moment I was ready to draw blade."

"Jest, is it?" Barbados cried, lurching forward almost to the foot of the table. "'Twill be considered no jest when we have stripped you of your jewels and plaything swords and this house of what valuables it contains! Back up against that wall, *señores,* and the man who makes a rash move will not live to make another!"

"I have made a multitude of rash moves, and I still live," Don Audre Ruiz told him. "Diego, it is indeed an excellent jest! I give you my thanks!"

"Pirates!" Don Diego said, laughing again. "In reality, I did not hire them to come here and furnish us with this entertainment. But since they have been so kind, it is no more than right that I pay them!" He sprang to his feet, bent forward with his hands upon the table, and glared down the length of it at Barbados. "You are the chief bull pirate?" he asked.

"I am the king of the crew!" Barbados replied. "Back against that wall, you and your friends!"

Don Diego Vega laughed lightly again. And then the laughter fled his face, and his eyes narrowed and seemed to send forth flakes of steel.

"*Sí!* You must be paid!" he said. "But there are many ways of making payment!"

The sword of Señor Zorro was beneath his hands. And suddenly it was out of its scabbard, and he had sprung upon the table and had dashed down the full length of it, scattering goblets and plates, drink and food.

Off the other end he sprang, and struck the floor a few feet in front of Barbados, who had recoiled and was struggling to get his cutlass out of his belt. The sword of Zorro flashed through the air, describing a gleaming arc.

"Pirate, eh?" Don Diego Vega cried. "You have come to collect riches, have you, Señor Pirate?"

"What is to prevent?" Barbados sneered. "You and your pretty toy of a sword?"

"Ha! You insult a good blade!" Don Diego cried. "The insult shall not go unpunished! Look you here!"

Don Diego Vega whirled suddenly to one side, his sword seemed to flash fire, and its point bit into a panel of the wall once, twice, thrice! Barbados looked on in amazement, his lower jaw sagging. His little eyes bulged, and he looked again. Scratched on the panel of the wall was a Z.

"That mark!" the pirate gasped. "You are Zorro! That mark—the same the *commandante* wears on his forehead—"

Don Diego had whirled to face him again. "How know you there is such a mark on the forehead of Captain Ramón?" he demanded. "So! The *commandante* deals with pirates, does he? That is how it happens that my friend, Sergeant Gonzales, and his soldiers are not here! Ha!"

Barbados blustered forward, his cutlass held ready, striving to regain the mastery of the situation. "Give us loot, or we attack!" he thundered.

"Attack, fool?" Don Diego cried. "Do you imagine that you hold the upper hand here? Up with your blade!"

The last thing Barbados wished to do was to fight a *caballero* under such circumstances. He had the fear of the mongrel for the thoroughbred. But here was a thing that could not be avoided unless his leadership of the pirates suffer.

The *caballeros* sprang from their chairs, drawing their swords, shouting in keen anticipation of a break in the deadly monotony of their lives. They rushed to the right and the left, and engaged the pirates as they rushed forward. Don Diego Vega found himself at liberty to engage Barbados only, a thing he relished and which he did with right good will.

Barbados fought like a fiend, mouthing curses, puffing out his cheeks, but he did not understand this style of fighting. Don Diego Vega seemed to be wielding half a dozen blades that sang about his head and threatened to bury themselves in his throat. His cutlass seemed heavy, useless, his strokes went wild.

Back toward the wall went Barbados, while Don Diego grinned at him and taunted him, played with him as a cat does with a mouse.

"Pirate, eh?" Don Diego said. "Terrible on either land or sea? 'Tis a jest, Señor Pirate! A thin jest!"

Barbados sensed that the termination of this combat was not to be to his liking. He got a chance to glance once around the big room. What he saw staggered him. Two of the *caballeros* were stretched on the floor, blood flowing from their wounds. But, aside from those two, the *caballeros* were getting much the better of the combat. The pirates were retreating toward the front door. Their heavy cutlasses were of no avail against flaming, darting light swords, especially when the men who handled those swords refused to stand and be cut down, but danced here and there like phantoms.

But Barbados did not have time to contemplate the scene long. Don Diego Vega pressed his attack. Back against the wall went the pirate chief. He crouched, fought his best. But suddenly he felt a twinge of pain in his wrist, and his cutlass left his hand and shot through the air, to fall with a crash in a corner.

Barbados stared stupidly before him and then came alive to his immediate peril. For Don Diego Vega was standing before him, smiling a smile that was not good to see.

"Payment shall be made!" Don Diego said.

His blade darted up and forward, and Barbados gave a little cry of pain and fear and recoiled. On his forehead, it seemed, was a streak of fire. Again the sword of Zorro darted forth, and there was a second streak of fire, and yet a third time. And then Don Diego Vega took a step backward and bowed mockingly.

"You wear my brand," he said. "It is an honor."

Terror had claimed Barbados for the moment. Now he slipped a short distance along the wall, while Diego followed him, and suddenly he shrieked his commands and darted toward the door. Into the plaza tumbled the pirates, with the *caballeros* at their heels.

Barbados shrieked more commands, and the pirates ran with what speed they had. Those left behind in the plaza gathered the horses they needed and the loot, and those coming from the *casa* of Don Diego rushed toward the horses now. For the greater part, those horses were fine-blooded stock and belonged to Don Diego's guests, mounts used to traveling at a rapid rate of speed between some *hacienda* and the town.

Barbados urged his men to haste. Only compact loot could be carried. They sprang to the backs of the horses and dashed away. The *caballeros* pursued on foot until the plaza had been crossed. And then they stopped and gathered around Don Diego.

"There can be no pursuit," Diego said. "They have made away with your horses, my friends, the soldiers are not here, and the only mounts remaining in town are not fit for *caballeros* to ride."

"Yet they must be pursued," said a voice at his side.

Don Diego whirled to find ancient Fray Felipe standing there.

"They have stolen the sacred goblet," Fray Felipe said in a calm voice. "I have taken a vow to regain it."

"The goblet!" Diego gasped.

"Don Diego, my friend, you will help me in this?" Fray Felipe asked. "I have known you since you were a babe in arms. I have loved you—"

"To-morrow I wed," Don Diego said. "But I shall do everything in my power. We'll get horses as soon as possible and pursue. I'll open my purse, and up and down El Camino Real men will go, seeking where these pirates touch shore again. We'll get the goblet!"

"I have more faith in your sword arm than in your purse, my friend," Fray Felipe said. "But do what you can."

The *caballeros* had gathered now. Men and women were pouring from the houses, telling of what had befallen them. Barbados and his men had been merciful, for pirates. They had taken wealth, but they had taken few lives.

Don Diego Vega started back across the plaza toward his house, his friends around him.

"For a moment I was Señor Zorro again," he said. "Those drops of blood you mentioned grew hot for a time, Audre, my friend."

"Glorious!" Audre Ruiz breathed. "I would we had horses and could follow them—even a ship to follow them out to sea. Don Diego, my friend, your bachelor supper is a great success."

"Then let us return and conclude it," Don Diego said. "We have a couple of wounded friends in the house. Let us attend them."

"Let us bathe their wounds in wine," Audre suggested.

They hurried into the house. The frightened servants came forward again and began putting things to rights. The two wounded *caballeros* were in chairs already, and men working to bandage them. Once more Don Diego sat at the head of the table, and the *caballeros* dropped into their chairs, and the servants made haste to fill the goblets. Don Diego put the sword of Zorro on the table before him and proposed that they toast it again.

There came a sudden commotion at the door, and a man stumbled in. Don Diego was on his feet instantly, for he knew the man. He was a leading workman at the *hacienda* of Don Carlos Pulido. A horrible fear gripped Don Diego's heart.

The man was exhausted. He staggered forward, and would have fallen had not Diego grasped him and braced him against a corner of the table.

"*Señor!*" he gasped. "Don Diego—young master!"

"Speak!" Diego commanded.

"Pirates attacked the *hacienda* more than an hour ago, while others were attacking here—"

"Tell it quickly!"

"Don Carlos is sorely wounded, *señor*! Many of the buildings are burned. The house was looted!"

"The *señorita*?" Don Diego questioned.

"Do not strike me when I speak, young master!"

"Speak!"

"They carried away the *señorita*. They slew six who would have saved her—"

"Carried her away!" Don Diego cried.

"Toward the sea," the man gasped. "I heard one of the pirates shout that she was to be treated gently—that she was to be the prize of some great man—"

Don Diego Vega tossed him aside, and once more the blade of Zorro was in his hand. His friends were upon their feet and crowding forward.

"A rescue!" Don Audre Ruiz cried. "We must save the *señorita*!"

"They have stolen the bride of Don Diego, the fools!" another shouted.

"Worse than that, for them!" Audre screeched. "They have stolen the bride of Señor Zorro!"

Don Diego Vega seemed to recover from the shock.

"You are right, my friends!" he cried. "This is touch enough to turn my blood hot again. Don Diego Vega is dead for a time; Señor Zorro takes the trail! Audre, get me the best horse you can! You others, wait!"

He dashed up the stairs as Audre hurried through the front door. The others waited, talking wildly of plans for reaching the shore of the sea. Frightened servants stood about as though speechless.

In a short space of time Don Diego returned to them. But he was Don Diego no longer. Now he wore the costume he had worn when as Señor Zorro he had ridden up and down the length of El Camino Real. And in his face was a light that was not good to see.

Don Audre hurried in. "I've got one good horse," he said.

"I go!" Don Diego cried. "I follow them to the sea. The two forces will meet there."

"We are with you in this!" Don Audre cried. "With you as when you were Zorro before. With you, my friend, until we have the little *señorita* safe again!"

Their naked blades flashed overhead in token of allegiance.

Don Diego thanked them with a look.

"Then follow me to the sea!" he cried. "A trading ship is due there in the morning. Mayhap we'll have to take it and trace them across the waves. I go! Zorro takes the trail!"

He dashed to the door, the others following. He sprang into the saddle of the mount Don Audre had procured. He drove home the spurs cruelly, and rode like a demon through the bright moonlight and up the slope, then taking the shortest trail to the sea.

SIX
ZORRO STRIKES

AT THE *HACIENDA* of Don Carlos Pulido the outer door was opened slowly, stealthily. A villainous face showed. Then the door was thrown open wide and half a dozen men stormed into the room. Doña Catalina gave a shriek of fear and sprang backward, and as the little *señorita* rushed to her, clasped her in her arms. Don Carlos looked up quickly from a garment he had been inspecting and sprang to his feet.

"Pirates!" he roared.

The aged don seemed to renew his youth with the cry. He darted back against the wall, shrieking for his servants and his men, his hand darting to the blade that happened to be at his side. But the surprise was complete, and there was no hope of a victory over the pirate crew. Servants rushed in loyally, to be cut down. Doña Catalina and Lolita crouched in a corner, the aged don standing protectingly before them.

Sanchez made for him, seeing the girl. The pirate laughed, attacked like a fiend, and Don Carlos went down before he could give a wound.

Doña Catalina's shriek rang in his ears. Then there came another shriek as Señorita Lolita felt herself being torn from her mother's arms. Sanchez whirled her behind him, and another of the pirates clutched her in his arms.

"Easy with the wench!" Sanchez cried. "She is to be saved for some great man!"

The little *señorita* struggled and fought, her gentleness gone in the face of this emergency. Horror claimed her and almost destroyed her reason. She had heard whispered wild tales of what happened to women captured by pirates.

Out of the house she was carried, shrieking in her fear. The pirates poured out, too. Some of the outbuildings were ablaze now, and the shrieking, swearing crew was looting the house for what valuables could be carried easily.

Men of the *hacienda* came running, to be cut down with a laugh. More huts were set ablaze. Pirates came running from the house, carrying jewels, silks, satins. Señorita Lolita realized dimly that her wedding garments had been ruined by these men.

"Diego!" she moaned. "Diego!"

Horses were procured, her father's blooded stock, and she was lashed to the back of one. The pirates mounted others, and Sanchez urged them on their way toward the distant sea. He had orders to get there before the dawn, and he feared Barbados too much to disobey his orders.

Señorita Lolita glanced back once, to see flames pouring from the doors and windows of the home she had loved. She thought of the father she had seen cut down, of her tender mother. And then she slumped forward in a swoon, and Sanchez steadied her in the saddle.

Two men of the *hacienda* carried Don Carlos Pulido from his burning home and placed him down at a distance beneath a tree. Doña Catalina knelt beside him, weeping.

"Find a horse!" the aged don commanded one of the men. "Ride like a fiend to the town, and tell Don Diego Vega of this. As you love the *señorita*, spare neither yourself nor your mount! Ride—do not bother with me!"

And so the man found a horse and rode away toward the town, going like the wind, and so the news came to Don Diego Vega.

The *señorita*, coming from her swoon, found that the pirates were traveling at a high rate of speed. Mile by mile they cut down the distance to the sea. There was an excellent trail used by traders, and Sanchez followed it swiftly.

It was like a nightmare to the little *señorita*. Again she wondered at the fate of her father and her mother. Again, mentally, she called upon Don Diego Vega to save her.

But her proud blood had returned to her now. She curled her pretty lips in scorn when Sanchez addressed her, and would make no reply. Her eyes snapped and flashed as she contemplated him. Her tiny chin tilted at an insulting angle. She was a Pulido, and she remembered it. Whatever fate held in store for her, she would be a Pulido to the end.

And finally, after some hours, they rounded a bend of a hill and saw the sea ahead of them, and the mouth of the dark cañon that ran down into it. Sanchez dismounted them beside the curving cliff. The loot was piled on the sand, the horses were turned adrift. Señorita Lolita was forced to dismount. Her wrists were lashed behind her, and she was compelled to sit on the ground with her back to the cliff's wall.

Some of the pirates lighted a fire of driftwood. Sanchez stood looking out to sea, watching for the ship that soon would be due.

And then came Barbados and the pirates from the town.

"Fair loot!" Barbados cried as Sanchez questioned. "But we were outdone. Some devilish *caballeros* were having a supper, and we stumbled upon them, twice our number. But we have fair loot! And you have the girl!"

"*Sí!* We have the girl!" Sanchez replied.

Barbados walked over to her. "A pretty wench!" he declared. "Small wonder a man wished to have you stolen! Proud, are you? Ha! We'll see what pride you have remaining by the end of the next moon!"

He whirled to look over the camp. "Sanchez," he commanded, "put a sentinel up on top of the cliff. I do not expect pursuit, but it is best to be prepared. I ran across that fiend of a Zorro, and he marked me. But there are not horses enough left in town for himself and his friends, and he would not dare follow alone. Nevertheless, put a sentinel on the cliff."

Sanchez obeyed. A man mounted to the top. On the level stretch of sand before them they could see his shadow in the moonlight as he paced slowly back and forth. Back and forth he went, while Señorita Lolita sat and watched the shadow and shivered to think of what was to come.

Barbados and Sanchez prepared the loot for the ship's boats when they should come. There was an abundance of wine, and the pirates began drinking it. They shouted and laughed and sang, while the little *señorita* shuddered and watched the shadow of the sentinel as it went back and forth, back and forth.

And suddenly she bent forward, for there were two shadows now. Hope sang in her breast. One of the shadows was creeping upon the other.

"Diego!" she breathed. "If it could only be Diego!"

The moon was dropping, was at the point where the shadows were lengthened, grotesque. And suddenly Sanchez gave a cry and pointed to the stretch of sand. Barbados turned to look. The pirates stopped drinking and crowded forward.

There on the sandy stretch a picture was being enacted. They saw the silhouettes of two men fighting, thrusting and slashing at each other. From above came the ringing of blades that met with violence.

The pirates sprang back, tried to look up and ascertain what was taking place there. The shadows disappeared from the sand for a time as the combatants reeled back from the edge of the cliff.

"Above, some of you!" Barbados cried.

They started—and stopped. Down the face of the cliff came tumbling the body of the pirate sentinel. It struck the sand, and Barbados and the others crowded forward to see.

"By the saints!" Barbados swore.

His little eyes bulged. On the cheek of the dead pirate sentinel was a freshly-carved Z.

"Barbados! Look!" Sanchez cried.

He pointed to the body. Fastened to the man's belt with a thorn was a scrap of parchment.

Barbados went forward gingerly and plucked it off. On it were words, evidently traced in blood with the point of a blade. Barbados read them swiftly:

Señores! Have you ever seen this one?

SEVEN
SEÑOR ZORRO'S DARING

THERE WAS a moment of horrified silence, during which nothing was heard save the soft lap of the sea against the shore and the labored breathing of the terrified pirates. And then Barbados swore a great oath and looked toward the summit of the cliff once more.

"'Tis that cursed Señor Zorro, the land pirate!" he shrieked. "Spit upon him! After him, dogs! Bring me his heart on the end of a cutlass blade! Or fetch him alive, if you can, that we may have the keen pleasure of killing him slowly."

Some of the pirates already were struggling to get up the narrow path that led to the top of the cliff, slipping and falling back as the soft soil and gravel rolled beneath their feet.

Sanchez started with them, eager for combat. Barbados, however, lingered behind, seeing to the loot and his fair prisoner. He was very busy about it, for he was not eager to join the others and run chances of matching blades with Señor Zorro again.

Barbados remembered well how he had felt during the fight in the house of Don Diego in Reina de Los Angeles, when he had realized fully that Don Diego was merely playing with him and could have silenced him forever when he willed.

The pirates reached the summit finally, but could see nothing there save a few clumps of brush and a few stunted trees that looked grotesque in the bright light of the moon. They examined the shadows carefully, but located no man. Yet from the near distance came a ringing, a mocking laugh.

They would have pursued, but Barbados hailed them from below, ordering them down to the beach again. The boats were putting in from the ship.

Down to the strand they tumbled, getting ready to store away their loot. They did not bother about the dead pirate, since he was an ordinary fellow who did not count. They guzzled more wine, ran down into the surf to help drag the boats ashore, greeted their fellows, laughed and shouted and jested and cursed in raucous tones.

Barbados turned to where the Señorita Lolita was sitting with her back against the cliff wall, her tiny wrists lashed behind her. She raised her face and looked at him bravely, her black eyes snapping, her lips curled in scorn.

"This Señor Zorro, I have been given to understand, has some concern in you," Barbados said.

"If he has, Señor Pirate, it is time for you to feel afraid," she replied.

"Think you that I fear the fellow? Ha!"

"He is no fellow! He is a *caballero* with the best of blood flowing in his veins, if you can understand what that means—you, who have the blood of swine in yours!"

"By my naked blade!" Barbados swore. "Were you not to be saved for a great man, I'd punish you well for that remark, proud one! Pride of blood, eh? Ha! 'Tis a thing you will be willing to forget, and eager, within a moon's time. When this man of whom I speak—"

"Is it necessary to speak at all to me?" the little *señorita* wanted to know.

Barbados snorted his anger and disgust. For a moment he turned away to issue a volley of commands to the men who were loading the boats. He berated Sanchez for being slow. He glanced up the face of the cliff once more, as though expecting Señor Zorro to come rushing down, deadly sword in hand. Presently he called two of his men to him.

"Take the wench to one of the boats!" he commanded. "Keep her wrists lashed. Make certain that she does not hurl herself into the sea. These high-born wenches have some queer ideas and are not to be trusted at a time such as this."

The two men grasped her roughly and forced her to her feet. The *señorita* gave a little cry, more because of her injured dignity than from pain or fear. Barbados whirled toward them again, anger in his face.

"Easy with the wench!" he commanded. "She is a proper and valuable share of the loot. If she is delivered in good condition then do we share greater in the other things."

Down to the edge of the hissing surf they went, Señorita Lolita Pulido forced along between them. She still held her head proudly, but the light of the dying fire reflected in her face showed a trace of glistening tears that could not be choked back. Still, she had some hope. Don Diego was near at hand! He already had demonstrated his presence. And he would not entirely desert her while he lived. He could be expected to play Señor Zorro now to the end of the chapter.

They lifted her, carried her between them, and put her down into one of the boats. She sat at one side of a middle seat, a wide thwart. Her bound wrists were over the side, and by turning slightly she could see the tossing water less than two feet below her, for the craft was heavily loaded.

The pirates tumbled into the boat and picked up the oars. One thrust her cruelly against the side. Barbados himself sprang in last of all and ordered his men to give way. The other boats prepared for the start also.

On the summit of the cliff Don Diego Vega crouched and watched them. But he was not the easy-going, fashionable, nonchalant Don Diego now. His eyes were narrowed and piercing. His lips were set in a thin, straight line. Don Diego had vanished, and in his place was Señor Zorro, the Fox, the man who had ridden up and down El Camino Real to avenge the wrongs of *frailes* and natives. And Señor Zorro would know how to deal with this grievous wrong, which touched him personally.

The pirate craft was anchored close inshore. It would not take long for the boats to reach her. The moon was sinking and soon would be gone. There would be but a brief period of darkness before the dawn came stealing across the land to the sea.

His *caballero* friends were far behind him, he knew. And they would make for the trading schooner anchored a few miles away, perhaps, instead of coming here. And Señorita Lolita Pulido was in the hands of the pirates, and expected to be rescued.

Señor Zorro realized these things even as he watched the pirates preparing to launch their boats. It did not take him long to make a decision. He crawled backward a short distance, sprang to his feet, and ran to the edge of the cliff in a little cove a few yards away, a spot the pirates could not see from their boats.

He made certain that his sword was fast in its scabbard. He tightened his belt. He went to the edge and glanced down at the hissing sea a score of feet below, where it rolled and eddied in a deep pool close to the rocks.

Back he went again. And suddenly he darted forward, took off at the very edge, and curved gracefully through the moonlight in a perfect dive.

He struck the water and disappeared, but in a moment he was at the surface and swimming away from the treacherous shore. And he found that it was treacherous and the tide an enemy. It pulled at him to drag him down. He fought and struggled against it, and finally won to safety.

The boats were just starting from the land. Señor Zorro, low in the water, swam as though in a contest for a prize, straight toward the nearest of the boats, which was the one in which the *señorita* was sitting a captive.

Señorita Lolita was struggling now to be brave. The pirates were singing their ribald songs and indulging in questionable jests. They swore as they tugged at the oars, cursed the heavy load of loot, and blasphemed because of the work they were forced to do.

The *señorita,* remembering her proud blood, had tried to maintain her courage, but now she felt it ebbing swiftly. There seemed to be no hope. She could not believe that Don Diego could come to her rescue in the face of such terrible odds. Once she gulped and felt herself near to tears. She leaned backward to keep as far as possible from the pirate sitting beside her. The stench of his body and breath was almost more than she could endure.

Now they were halfway to the pirate ship. Lolita had arrived at a decision. She would be no prey for pirates if she could find at hand the means for taking her own life. She remembered what Barbados had said about her being the prize of some great man, and wondered at it a bit. But suppressed terror occupied her mind and kept her from wondering much. Again she leaned backward, and her bound hands almost touched the water over the side.

The pirates, nearing exhaustion, were rowing slowly now, sweeping their long oars in unison but without their usual force. And suddenly the Señorita Lolita flinched, and almost cried aloud, then struggled to overcome the shock she had felt. Her hands had been touched.

At first she thought it was some monster of the sea, and then that a cold wave had washed them. But the touch came again, and she knew it for what it was—the touch of another hand.

Another touch—and her cheeks flamed scarlet. The *señorita* had had her hands kissed before, and she knew a kiss when she felt it.

She turned her head slowly, leaning outward, and glanced down. And her heart almost stood still.

For Señor Zorro was there, his face showing just at the surface of the water! Don Diego, her husband-to-be, was there, swimming alongside, smiling up at her, within a few feet of the pirates who bent their backs and rowed and never thought to look down.

Fear clutched at the *señorita's* heart for an instant—fear for him—yet admiration for his daring, too. Her blood seemed suddenly hot instead of cold. The touch of his lips had been enough to do that.

He dared not speak, of course, though the pirates were shouting and singing. But his lips moved and formed voiceless words, and the *señorita* understood.

"Courage! I'll be near!" he mouthed.

She nodded her head slightly in token that she understood. And Don Diego Vega smiled yet again and sank slowly out of sight beneath the waves.

The boats were almost to the vessel now. The bright moon shipped a last ray across the tumbling sea and sank to rest. On the deck of the pirate craft torches flared suddenly to guide the boats.

They reached the side. Rough hands lifted the *señorita* and forced her to the deck above. Swearing, sweating men commenced handing up the loot. Barbados howled his commands and curses, Sanchez echoing them. To one side the *señorita* was held by the two men who had guarded her on the shore, awaiting disposition by the pirate chief.

"With speed, dogs!" Barbados shrieked. "We must be away before the dawn!"

The entire crew was working amidships, getting in the plunder and the boats. They gave no thought to bow or stern.

And up the anchor chain and into the bow crept a dripping figure, with a cry for vengeance in his heart—and the sword of Zorro at his side!

PART TWO

PART II

EIGHT
THE GOBLET

SEÑORITA LOLITA PULIDO, after a time, was conducted by Barbados to a tiny cabin below decks. It was no more than eight feet square, and had a bunk along one side of it. Certainly, it was no place for a delicately-reared lady of gentle blood.

It was far from being clean, in the first instance. Vermin that meant nothing to pirates caused the *señorita* to shudder and almost scream. Even as she entered, two huge rats scampered through a hole in the cabin floor, rushed down into the bowels of the ship.

"'Tis no palace," Barbados admitted. "I'll leave the torch so you may have light until the day dawns, which will not be long. The torch will keep the rats away. The smoke will drift through that open porthole. You will be safe here. There are no weapons, and even such a small and dainty tender human being as yourself cannot squeeze through that porthole and drop into the open sea!"

The *señorita* had no reply for him. She tilted her chin again, tried to hum a little song, and glanced around the tiny place. Barbados grew surly.

"Too good to speak to me, are you, proud one?" he sneered. "You may have another tune to chant before many days, after you have met the man for whom you were stolen. Is there anything you want or need?"

The *señorita's* face flushed, but she faced him bravely. "I want your absence —and deeply feel the need of it!" she replied.

"By my naked blade! Were it not that you are to be handed over to another, I'd take it upon myself to tame you!" Barbados declared. "Ha! Deliver me from proud wenches with their noses in the air!"

He fastened the smoking torch to a wall, went out and slammed the door behind him, and Señorita Lolita heard a heavy bar being dropped into place. For a moment she stood in the middle of the cabin, her hands clutching spasmodically at her breast, and then she went over to the bunk, inspected it, and finally crawled upon it and sat cross-legged, staring at the opposite wall.

The ship was old, the floor worn and full of holes, and the walls had cracks in them. From one side came a stench, as though supplies had been stored in the space adjoining, and had spoiled. Through the porthole she could see the black night.

The horror of her situation was heavily upon her now. She seemed to fully realize her predicament for the first time. She remembered again how she had seen her father cut down, and her home in flames. She wondered how it fared with her parents, and she wondered, too, what was to be in the future.

The only ray of hope was that Don Diego was near, that Señor Zorro had promised to give her aid, and that his sword would protect her. And yet how could he—one man against scores of scoundrels? Don Diego, even as Señor Zorro, was only human, after all. Yet she hoped that, at the climax, he would reveal himself. He was a *caballero*, and he would know what to do in an emergency. Better that Señor Zorro drive his blade through her heart than for her to live stained!

She heard a tumult on the deck, a great noise, the sounds of clanking chains, and knew from the feel of the ship that she was under sail. Above her head feet pattered on the deck. The great voice of Barbados and the echoing one of Sanchez came to her as from a long distance. The rushing wind pulled the smoke of the torch through the open porthole.

The *señorita* sighed and leaned her head against the wall of the cabin. Tears trickled from her eyes and started coursing down her cheeks, but she wiped them away swiftly. None of these pirates should see her cry! Never would they be able to say that one of the blood of the Pulidos had shown fear!

She closed her eyes for an instant, as though that would shut out the horror of her thoughts, but found that it did not. It seemed to her that she heard a faint hiss, but she supposed that it was the wind or the water.

She opened her eyes again—and almost shrieked in alarm. Four inches in front of her face the point of a sword had slipped through a tiny crack in the wall, coming from the space adjoining!

The *señorita* recoiled a space, but watched the blade as though fascinated by it. Inch by inch it slipped through the wall, until two-thirds of its length was inside the cabin. And again she restrained a cry, but this time a cry of joy. On the blade, marked with some black substance, was a big Z!

So Señor Zorro even now was near! He was on the other side of the partition, only a couple of feet from her! She bent her head forward as the blade was slowly withdrawn, put her lips close to the tiny crack in the wall.

"Diego!" she whispered.

"Not Diego, but Señor Zorro, *señorita,* at your service," came back a low tone.

"Thank the saints!" she breathed. "But, what can you do? You must be careful!"

"Think you I would allow them to carry you away, and not follow?" he asked.

"If they find you—"

"Do you put such small value, *señorita,* upon my ability to care for myself?"

"Diego! Zorro!" she whispered. "To you I am not backward in confessing it —I am so afraid!"

"Then will I sing for you, beloved!"

"Zorro! Dare not to do it! They may hear!"

"Let them hear a decent song for once in their wicked lives!" Señor Zorro said. "Be of strong heart, *señorita*! And be not frightened at what you may hear or see. It is in my mind to terrorize these vermin who call themselves men, preparatory to rescuing you!"

"Brave words, Diego!" she said. "But you cannot fight against four score. If, at the end, you could do me one service—"

"And that?" he asked.

"Death is to be preferred to dishonor, Diego!"

"Why speak of dying? Do you forget that you are my affianced bride? You are to live, and I am to live, *señorita,* and have many happy years. Think always on that, and not on the other! And be of good cheer, for I am near you always!"

She heard a slight movement on the other side of the partition. He did not speak again, nor did she. Her heart was beating like angry waves against a rocky shore. Her face was flushed. It gave her courage just to know that he was near. Señor Zorro, she felt confident, would find a way.

There was silence for a moment, and then she heard the soft hiss again.

"*Sí?*" she questioned.

"This is some sort of a storeroom," he said, "in which Zorro has made a temporary nest. But I do not intend to remain in it forever. It is in my mind to look at you through the porthole before the dawn comes."

"Diego! To dare such a thing—"

"What would not a *caballero* dare for love?" he asked. "For love of such a one—"

"Diego!"

"Call me Zorro, for, by the saints, that is my rôle now! I find that I have a dual personality, and the tamer part of me is not working at present. I am Zorro, the daring in love and war!"

"Have a care, for my sake," she begged.

"I have work to do and a game to play, and they may be combined," he answered. "For the moment, *Adios*!"

Again she heard the little sound, as though he were retreating from the partition and crawling over boxes and bales. There was deep silence for a time, save for the noises on the deck. And then she heard his voice, raised in song, and her heart almost stopped, for she knew that the pirates must hear it, too.

She leaned her head against the wall, that she might hear the better, though she was sorely afraid. She had heard the song often before, from Don Diego's lips, and when other young *caballeros* had come to her father's *hacienda* serenading. But never had she heard the real Señor Zorro sing it before, and never before had it sounded so thrilling and so sweet.

"*Atención!* A *caballero's* near!
To guard the one to his heart most dear!
To love, to fight, to jest, to drink!
To live the life and never shrink!
His blade is bright, his honor, too!
Atención!"

The voice grew louder, more ringing. It seemed to the *señorita* to swell through the ship and across the tossing sea. Her heart beat faster, though she still feared for him. Well she knew the audacity, the reckless courage of her Señor Zorro!

"Zorro!" she breathed. "Man of men! *Caballero* mine!"

There was silence on the deck above, and then she heard the harsh, loud voice of Barbados, but could not understand his words. Señor Zorro was continuing his song:

"*Atención!* I've a thrust in store
For rogues, for foes, an abundance more
To shield my lady from all harm,
To save her from the world's alarm;
A *caballero* calls to you—
Atención!"

The *señorita's* eyes closed, her lips parted slightly, her breathing became as the stirring of a leaf in a gentle breeze. The song had lulled her fears.

"Zorro!" she whispered, as the verse was ended. But there came no answer from the other side of the partition.

Up on the deck, however, there was consternation. Barbados, having listened, whirled angrily toward his crew.

"Who dares sing such a song?" he shrieked. "Are there not royally good pirate ditties, that some of you must use the mush-like tunes and words of the high-born?"

"Every man is on deck," wailed Sanchez, who had been superintending the storing of the loot. "'Tis a ghost song!" he exclaimed.

"A ghost song!" shrieked some of those nearest him.

Barbados shuddered. "There will be ghosts aplenty if this nonsense does not stop!" he declared, whipping his cutlass out of his belt. "It was no ghost singing. A ghost would have a more perfect voice. If I hear it again—"

He heard it again. It seemed to come from the sails above, from the waves overside, from the cabins below.

"*Dios!*" Barbados swore. "By my naked blade—"

"It is a ghost song!" Sanchez whimpered again.

Barbados whirled upon him, but the lieutenant dodged the blow that would have hurled him senseless to the deck. The pirate chief, breathing heavily, looked around at his men. Terror already had claimed some of them.

"It is a trick of some scurvy knave I'll split in twain!" he declared. "On with your work!"

The men shivered, but again bent to their tasks. Barbados walked to the rail and stood looking down at the dark water, and then toward the land, where the dawn was almost due. Through the darkness and up to him slipped one of the pirate crew.

"Master!" he whispered.

"To your work, hound of hell!"

"A word with you, master!"

"Concerning what?" Barbados demanded.

The man edged closer. "Master, I have a present for you—a goodly piece of loot that is not in the common store."

"How is this?" Barbados said. "You steal from your comrades?"

"Softly, master, else they hear!" the man whispered. "This is something special, and I got it for you."

"In Reina de Los Angeles?"

"*Sí*, master! In Reina de Los Angeles. It was while we were in the church there."

"In the church?" Barbados gasped.

"When the old *fray* first stood us off, master, and before you came. We had rushed forward, and I was in the van. And when the old *fray* was hurled backward the first time, I got it."

"And what is it?"

"A golden goblet, master, studded with precious gems. See—I have it here!

I saved it for you, master, and thought perhaps that you might give me promotion—"

Barbados looked at the goblet, struck by the light from the nearest torch. It glowed and glistened like some live thing. The pirate chief recoiled.

"Away with it!" he cried. "I do not want to touch it—do not wish to see it! It is a thing of ill-omen, the thing that old *fray* was trying to protect!"

"But, master—"

"Ill-luck will follow the man who has it. It is some sort of holy thing! Away with it! Keep it for yourself. Gamble it away, and the sooner you get rid of it the better. You may be struck down for taking it. I had a friend once who robbed a church and struck a priest, and I do not care to remember what happened to him! Are you going to take it away?"

The man gasped, astonished, and put the golden goblet beneath his shirt.

"I may have it all for myself?" he asked.

"*Sí!* I would not touch the thing! I call upon the saints to witness that I never touched it!"

So, through all the ages, have wicked men, in moments of fear, called upon the gods they have pretended to scorn.

NINE
LOVE AND MYSTERY

SEÑOR ZORRO, having concluded his song, crept over boxes and bales to the little door of the storeroom. There he crouched and listened for a time, but heard nothing save the noise from the ship's deck and the wash of the sea and singing of the wind through the rigging.

Presently he opened the door a crack and peered out into a pitch-dark, narrow passage. He slipped through and closed the door after him. Again he stopped to listen, and then he crept forward, reached a ramshackle ladder, and went up it swiftly and silently to a tiny hatch.

Lifting the hatch he crawled out upon the deck near the rail, hidden from the glare of all the torches. He had seen such a ship as this before, and knew her build well. There were no mysteries for him.

Along the rail he went like a shadow, and as silently. He reached a point where he could look amidships. Barbados was back among his men, now, urging them to greater speed, and Sanchez was echoing his commands. The ship was sailing at a fair rate of speed before a freshening breeze.

Señor Zorro crouched in the darkness and contemplated the pirate crew for a moment. He put out a hand to brace himself against the rolling of the vessel, and it came in contact with a tub of small bolts. Señor Zorro had an inspiration.

Far ahead of him, in the flare of a torch, he saw the ship's bell. Señor Zorro grasped one of the little bolts, stood to his feet, took careful aim, and hurled the bolt from the darkness. He missed the bell by the fraction of a foot, and the bolt flew overboard.

Señor Zorro grunted, got another bolt, and tried again. It struck the bell squarely, glanced away, and fell into the sea. Out above the din rang one clear note. The ship had an excellent bell.

Instantly there was silence. Barbados whirled to look forward. His crew stood open-mouthed.

"The ship's bell sounded!" Sanchez wailed.

"And which of you struck it?" Barbados demanded.

"No man was near it," Sanchez declared. "But it sounded. I do not like this business!"

Barbados shivered, but made a show of courage. "Something struck it," he said. "Possibly something dropped from aloft. Are you babies that you flinch because of the ringing of a bell? To your work, else I wade among you, naked blade in hand! Ha! I have sailed with a throng of children, it appears!"

They bent to their work again, and at that moment Señor Zorro hurled another bolt, and the bell rang out clearly once more. Again the work stopped as though Barbados had bawled an order for the men to cease.

"A ghost bell!" a man shrieked.

"A ghost bell!" Sanchez declared, crossing himself. "We are doomed! The ship is doomed!"

"To your work!" Barbados was both afraid and angry now. He strode forward, threatening them. He made his way toward the bell, and stood looking at it. Because of his presence the bell did not ring again. Yet Barbados did not feel at all easy. He beckoned the man who had the goblet.

"You retain the thing?" he asked.

"*Sí, señor!*"

"It is an evil thing for you to hold."

"You want it?"

"Not I, by the saints!" Barbados swore. "And do you keep away from me while the thing is in your possession. If misfortune comes to the ship or the company because of the goblet, then will you go overside first of all! And with a weight around your neck!"

The man scurried away along the deck, and Barbados, his courage returning, whirled around and issued a volley of commands. From the darkness Señor Zorro hurled another small bolt, and for the third time the bell sent forth its ringing message.

Barbados whirled around again, his face suddenly white. He was within six paces of the bell, and he knew that no other man was nearer it than that. He felt the eyes of the terror-stricken crew upon him, and knew that he must show courage now, else lose his control over his men.

"Some one is playing a trick," Barbados said. "And when I find the hound of hell who is doing it, I feed him to the sharks in two sections!"

He called two of the men, bade them get torches, and stationed them near the bell with orders to watch it closely. They shivered, but they obeyed. Thoughts of a ghost were terrible enough, but Barbados was there in the flesh, and his cutlass was ready in his hand.

But the bell did not ring again. Señor Zorro had accomplished his purpose, which was to make the crew nervous, and he was through playing in that direction. He slipped on along the rail, now and then peering over. After a time he picked up a line, fastened it to the rail and tossed the other end overboard, tried it with the weight of his body, made a loop in it, and slipped one leg through the loop.

Over the rail and down the side he went, slowly and carefully, the sword of Zorro in its scabbard at his side. And presently he came to a porthole, through which light streamed. He swung around, grasped the edge of it.

The Señorita Lolita, looking up suddenly, almost shrieked in sudden alarm. But the next instant she was off the bunk and across the tiny cabin, and her face was within a foot of his.

"Zorro!" she said. "You are doing a reckless thing—"

"Would I allow a few score mere pirates to keep us apart?" he asked. "Am I that sort of *caballero*?"

"But you are in grave danger, from the men above and the sea beneath!"

"Danger is the spice of life, *señorita*! After we are wedded it will be time enough for me to be tame."

"But that may never be, Diego."

"Zorro, *señorita,* if it is all the same to you. I must remember continually now that I am Zorro."

"You must get back to the deck and go into hiding," she said. "I fear for you. And should anything happen to you what would become of me?"

"It is some small risk," Señor Zorro admitted, "but I felt that I should make this call."

One of her hands was at the porthole's edge. Señor Zorro, clinging to the rope, grasped it in his right hand and carried it to his lips.

"The most beautiful *señorita* in all the world!" he said.

"Zorro!"

"And for once I have you, *señorita,* when your *duenna* is not present to pester us. We are betrothed. We were to have been wed to-day. I will have more courage, *señorita,* if I have felt your lips against mine. The memory of our betrothal kiss still tingles in my veins, but it is a memory that should be refreshed."

"Señor—"

"How is this?"

"Diego! Zorro, I mean!"

"That is much better."

"And then you will climb above and take heed for yourself?"

"With a kiss for incentive, I could climb to the summit of the world and reach for heaven!" Señor Zorro declared.

She blushed and then inclined her head. He bent forward, and their lips met in the porthole.

"Go!" she said then. "Go, Zorro, and may the saints guard you!"

"My arm is strengthened," he declared. "And your wishes are to be obeyed. *Señorita, adios!*"

An instant their eyes met, and then he was gone, climbing up the line hand over hand through the darkness. Señorita Lolita tried to watch him, but could not. And so she hurried back to the bunk and curled up on it again, holding one hand to her flaming cheek, moistening with her tongue the lips that the lips of Señor Zorro had pressed.

Zorro reached the deck and disconnected the line, wishing to leave no trace behind him. He glanced toward the land, and realized that soon the dawn would come. Along the rail he slipped, until he came to a spot from where he could watch the pirates.

The majority of the loot had been stored away. No man was aloft. Barbados was cursing at a group near the opposite rail. Señor Zorro looked across at him and wished that he was near. He saw Sanchez, too, knew him for the lieutenant, and it came into his mind that Sanchez had commanded the squad that had abducted the *señorita*.

And, as he watched, Sanchez started across the deck, around the mast, bore down upon Señor Zorro where he stood in the darkness. Soon he would be in the darkness near the rail. But before he could reach it he would be forced to pass beneath one of the flaring torches, and for an instant the strong light would be in his eyes. Señor Zorro whipped out his blade and crept forward to the edge of the blackness, keeping behind a mass of cordage piled upon the deck.

His eyes were narrowed now, his lips in a straight line, an expression of determination in his face. So he stood and watched Sanchez approach, holding the sword of Zorro ready.

The moment came. The blade darted forward and struck, and its point worked like lightning. Sanchez gave a scream of mingled surprise and pain and fear, and reeled backward, clapping a hand to his forehead.

Barbados whirled to look. Señor Zorro, as silently as a shadow, darted along the rail through the black night, on his way to the little hatch and the storeroom below.

"Fiends of hell!" Barbados was shrieking. "Sanchez, what is it? You screech like a shocked wench!"

Sanchez, still shrieking, staggered back and turned beneath the flaring torch to face them. On his forehead was a freshly cut letter Z.

"The mark of Zorro!" Barbados gasped. "So—"

"A demon struck me!" Sanchez cried. "I saw no man! Something came out of the night and struck me!"

"Fool!" Barbados shrieked. "A blade made those cuts."

"But there was no blade, no man! Out of the dark it came—"

"Think you Señor Zorro is aboard?"

"No man, I say!" Sanchez shrieked. "It was a ghost. There is a ghost aboard. We are doomed—the ship is doomed! The ship's bell rings—and men are cut—"

"By my naked blade!" Barbados swore. "A sword in the hand of a human made that cut! Do I not bear one myself?"

"But how could this Señor Zorro get aboard?" Sanchez wailed. "It was a ghost!"

The ship's bell gave forth one more melodious clang! Señor Zorro, on his way to the storeroom and his hiding place, had stopped long enough to hurl another bolt.

TEN
A DEAD PIRATE

SANCHEZ and some of the others shrieked in terror. Barbados, cursing loudly, strode to the middle of the deck, whirled around, brandished his cutlass as though he would have fought the world. He would not admit to himself that this thing was getting on his nerves, but he glanced anxiously toward the land and wished for the dawn. He drove the men to finish their work, grasped Sanchez roughly by the arm, and led him aside.

"Understand," he said, "either this Señor Zorro is aboard in some mysterious fashion, or else there is a traitor among us playing this Zorro's part."

"A ghost—" Sanchez began.

"Another word of ghosts, and I run you through!" Barbados warned. "The men are silly fools, but you are supposed to have some sense, being second in command. When the day comes we search the ship; and if we find this Señor Zorro in hiding we deal with him in a way he will not relish. He is one man against many!"

Sanchez shivered and raised a trembling hand to his flaming forehead. The blood had streamed down his cheeks from the wound Señor Zorro had put there; and Señor Zorro, on his way to his hiding place, had paused for an instant to watch this comedy—had paused, and so was lost to caution.

Back along the rail he hurried and from the tub he took some of the bolts. Up into the rigging he went like a monkey, until he was over the deck. He braced himself, took careful aim, and once more the bell rang out.

The pirates whirled toward it, and Barbados took a step forward, an oath rumbling from his lips, while Sanchez screeched and tried to hide behind the mast. Señor Zorro hurled another bolt, and this one struck Sanchez on his shoulder. He cried out again and fled across the deck.

Another bolt hurtled through the night, and this time Barbados felt the blow on the back of his neck. The screeches of Sanchez drowned the noise of the bolt falling to the deck. The pirate chief whirled upon the men nearest.

"Some one is playing tricks!" he shrieked. "If I find the man doing it—"

The bell rang again. It was too much for the pirates. They rushed toward the rail and stood there, white of face and shivering, clutching at their breasts, looking out into the black night as though they expected some demon to come riding toward them on a breath of breeze.

Señor Zorro went down the rigging swiftly, for the first streak of dawn was showing over the land and stealing across the sea. Along the rail he rushed, reached the little hatch, and let himself down. A few minutes later he was safe among his boxes and bales in the storeroom.

He crept across to the tiny crack through which he had whispered to the *señorita;* but he could not see her where she was sitting on the bunk—could see only straight ahead.

"*Señorita!*" he whispered.

"Zorro!"

"Safe again, *señorita*. I have been playing with these babies of pirates."

"Be not rash, else I call you Don Diego," she said.

"How can I be Señor Zorro, and not rash?" he wanted to know. "The dawn is coming. Have you rested?"

"I could not sleep," she replied. "There were thoughts of you, and of other things."

"But now I guard," he whispered. "Sleep, and I will watch."

She started to make reply, but instead she hissed a warning. Heavy steps had sounded outside the cabin door. She heard the bar being removed. And then the door was opened and one of the pirates stood in it, grinning, a torch in his hand.

"I have brought food," he said, "at the chief's command."

Señorita Lolita's lips curled in scorn as she looked at him.

"Do you think I would eat it?" she asked.

"It is the chief's command. You are to be kept well fed and pretty as the prize of some great man."

"You may take your food away again!"

"And have the chief slit my throat for not carrying out his orders?" the man asked. "Do you take me for a fool?"

He stepped into the little cabin and closed the door behind him. And then she saw that he carried a bottle of wine and half a cold fowl. She gasped as she looked at the wine, for there was a label upon the bottle, and it bore the stamp of her father's *hacienda*.

It returned to her with a rush—memory of her father being struck down, of her home in flames, of her weeping mother crouched over her father's body. She gave a little cry and reeled back against the wall.

"Leave me!" she commanded. "Out!"

The man leered and stepped toward her. She darted away from him, horror in her eyes. He put the bottle and fowl down upon the bunk.

"I leave the food and drink, pretty wench," he said. "You may use it or throw it through the porthole into the sea—it is all the same to me."

"Out!" she cried again.

"You do not like me?" he asked, getting closer to her. "Many women have. You are not to be spoiled being the prize of some great man, but a kiss will not spoil you. Never have I kissed a wench with proud blood in her veins. It will be something to remember and boast about!"

Now she crouched against the wall, her heart pounding at her ribs, her breath coming in little gasps. Her eyes were dilated with terror.

"Out!" she said, though her fear reduced her screech to a mere whisper. "Your master shall know of this!"

That sobered him for a moment, but the picture of her pretty self was before him, tantalizing him, tormenting him. He reached out a hand to clutch her. She could retreat no further. She put up her tiny hands as though to beat him back.

"What is a kiss?" he asked, laughing. "I would not harm you—only a kiss!"

"I would rather die!" she gasped.

"For that I shall take two—a dozen! Proud wench, are you? Ha!"

He grasped her wrist and started pulling her toward him. She lurched backward, fought with what strength she could, felt that she was about to swoon, and realized that she must not. He followed her, reached out the other hand to grasp her better.

And like the darting of a snake's tongue came the sword of Zorro through the crack in the wall. In and out it darted with the swiftness of thought. The *señorita*, reeling back against the wall, felt herself released, saw the pirate sag before her, to his knees, topple forward, and collapse at her feet.

Terror-stricken, she looked down at him, her eyes bulging wide. Blood flowed from his breast and formed a pool on the floor of the cabin. A hiss from the other side of the partition brought her to her senses. She realized, then, that Zorro's blade had done this thing to save her an indignity.

"Señorita!"

"*Sí?*" she questioned.

"Take the fellow's dagger from his girdle! Dip it in the blood on the floor! Have courage and act quickly! 'Twill appear as though you did it when he offered you insult!"

She realized what he meant, and was quick to obey. She needed the blood of the Pulidos to aid her now. Stooping, she reached out a hand and grasped the hilt of the dagger in the dead man's belt. She drew it out, shuddered, turned her head away for a moment, faint at the sight of the blood.

"Courage!" Zorro's whisper reached her ears. "And make haste, *señorita*! Some man may come!"

Now came the thing that tested her courage. But she felt that the eyes of Señor Zorro were upon her. Again she bent forward, and she bathed the blade of the dagger in the pool of blood upon the floor. Then she sprang to her feet, holding the dagger in her hand, her face white.

"Open the door," Zorro whispered from beyond the partition, "and shriek!"

She hurried to the door, shuddering as she pulled her skirts away from the dead man. She opened it, and peered out. And the shriek that she gave was no acting, but the sudden outpouring of what she felt.

There was a moment of silence, and she shrieked yet again. And down from the deck tumbled Barbados, rage in his face. He looked at her and at the dagger in her hand. He thrust her aside and stepped into the cabin.

"So!" he said. "What has happened here?"

"A lady of my blood does not suffer insult!" she said.

"Ha! The dog forgot his instructions, did he? 'Tis well that he is done for! You have saved me a task!" Barbados declared. He turned and looked full at her. "A wench of spirit!" he said. "I have half a mind to keep you for my own!"

Back to the door he went, and shouted to those above. Two men came rushing down. Barbados yelled commands at them, and they carried the dead man away. Another brought water in a pail, and dashed it over the floor to wash the blood down the cracks.

Barbados turned and looked at her again. "You may keep the beast's dagger for a souvenir," he said. "Let me clean it for you."

She surrendered it willingly. Barbados wiped the blade on his trousers, bowed, and handed it back to her.

"Take it!" he urged. "Use it when you will, if there are others who try to disobey my commands. You are to be delivered, unspoiled, to a certain man. Failing that, I claim you for myself. And put out the torch when I have gone. The day is here!"

He went out and closed the door, and once more the heavy bar was dropped into place. Señorita Lolita tossed the dagger from her, hurried to the bunk, and collapsed upon it. Her senses seemed to be reeling. She forgot to extinguish the torch.

"Señorita!" Zorro whispered from beyond the partition.

But she made him no reply. The terrors of the night had taken their toll. She had swooned at the dawning of the day.

ELEVEN
ZORRO WALKS THE PLANK

THERE WAS no dawn in the dark, evil-odored storeroom, but Señor Zorro, by peering through the crack and into the little cabin, could tell of the approach of the day. The interior grew gray, and then brighter, and finally a ray of sun penetrated and touched the dingy hole with glory.

Señor Zorro put his lips close to the tiny opening and whispered his call:

"*Señorita!*"

Her swoon had changed to a deep, unnatural slumber by now, and she came from the midst of it at his sibilant call, bewildered for a moment.

"*Sí?*" she asked.

"You were silent for a time, and I was afraid."

"Señor Zorro afraid?" she mocked.

"Afraid and not ashamed of it, where you are concerned, *señorita,*" he replied. "Curl up and try to get some natural sleep. It is in my mind that these pirates will be busy beating out to sea or trying to reach their land den, and will have no time to bother you."

"And what do you intend doing?" she asked. "Do you intend to sleep also?"

"Don Diego Vega might feel called upon to sleep now and then," he answered, "but Señor Zorro dare not. Worry not your pretty head about me, *señorita*! Rest your pretty eyes, and by the time you awake fate perhaps will have been kind and revealed to us a way out of this present difficulty."

She heard him scrambling among his boxes and bales and barrels. She would have spoken to him again, but did not dare raise her voice above a whisper, and she felt slumber claiming her. She was thoroughly exhausted. Before she went to sleep, however, she extinguished the torch, and stood for a moment before the open porthole, looking through the morning haze at the distant land.

The ship was riding easily on the long swells, sailing swiftly toward the south. The *señorita* slept, and in the dark storeroom Señor Zorro reclined on a pile of sacks and tried to think things out. In an emergency he was quick to think and to act, to take advantage of every opening, but to sit still and analyze a situation was beyond him. He was a man of action, and it was action he craved.

He did not doubt that Don Audre Ruiz and the others had obtained possession of the trading schooner and would follow. But would they follow the correct lane of the sea? And, if they caught up with the pirates, what would follow? The *caballeros* would be greatly outnumbered. Not that such a thing would cause them to hesitate about an attack, but it would work against them, of course.

For an hour or more Señor Zorro thought on the problem, itching to be in action and knowing that he should remain quiet. The pirates would be searching the ship, he supposed, since he had marked Sanchez the way he had. He would have to remain in hiding, bury himself in the storeroom in such manner that they could not find him.

Then, after a time, he heard a noise in the little cabin, and quickly made his way to the crack in the wall. He could see that the door had been opened, and then he saw that Sanchez was standing just inside it.

"*Señorita!*" the pirate lieutenant called. "Sleep not when the chief commands!"

Señorita Lolita came from her slumber and sat up on the bunk with a little cry.

"Do not be afraid," Sanchez told her. "By my naked blade, I will keep my distance! I have no wish for a knife between my ribs, driven there by a high-born damsel who thinks nothing of murder!"

"What is your wish?" she demanded. She was herself again now, scorning him, her chin tilted.

"It is no wish of mine," Sanchez protested. "I but carry the commands of the chief. He orders that you come on deck, and at once."

"I prefer to remain here, Señor Pirate," she replied.

"No doubt. But the commands of Barbados are made to be obeyed, as I learned some years ago. He has said that you are to go on deck, and so you shall, even if I have to carry you."

One step he took toward her, but she sprang from the bunk and crouched against the wall.

"Dare not to touch me, foul beast!" she cried. "'Twas you cut my father down! 'Twas you stole me away from my home and fetched me to the coast!"

"I do not want to touch you, little spitfire!" Sanchez informed her. "I have but come to escort you to the deck. What Barbados wants with you I do not know. Perhaps it is to have you get some fresh air, so you will look pretty when you are delivered to the great man. Ha! You are pretty enough now to suit any man who is not too exacting."

He turned back toward the door, offering her no affront. And there he waited, as though with deep respect.

"Are you coming?" he demanded. "Barbados is not the man to be kept waiting."

Once more she curled her lip in scorn, once more her chin was tilted, and she went forward, drawing aside her skirts, and swept past him like a queen leaving an audience chamber. Sanchez grinned and followed her.

Señor Zorro, through the tiny crack, had witnessed this scene. He did not believe that Barbados merely wanted her to take the air. He felt sudden fear for her, and once more his eyes narrowed and seemed to send forth flakes of steel. He scrambled over the boxes and bales toward the little door.

Up the rickety ladder he went and to the hatch, and there he listened for a time, hearing nothing alarming. And then he raised the hatch slowly, an inch at a time, blinking his eyes rapidly at the bright light of the day.

None of the pirates was in sight. Señor Zorro slipped out and dropped the hatch covering, whipped out his blade, and crept through the little passage toward the spot from where the deck of the ship could be viewed.

He was in time to see the *señorita* piloted across the deck to where Barbados was standing alone. The crew were forward, some sleeping sprawled on the deck, others leaning against the rail watching the antics of the flying fish.

Barbados whirled and stood with arms akimbo, regarding her narrowly. She faced him bravely, her hands clasped behind her back.

"*Señorita,*" the pirate said, "queer things happened during the night. I would question you concerning them."

"Is it necessary?" she asked.

"By my naked blade, it is!" he roared. "I am not to be treated like a dog by you or any of your ilk. This is my ship, and here I am sole master, and it would be well for you to remember it."

"I am quite sure none other would desire the mastery of her," the *señorita* replied.

"You have a biting tongue," Barbados said. "I would hate to be your husband. Else that tongue were tamed by love, it would be a hot dish to have continually."

She turned away from him and gazed across the sea. He took a step nearer her.

"Is this Señor Zorro aboard?" he demanded suddenly.

"Would I know it, were he?" she countered.

"Possibly. I am asking a question, and desire an answer," Barbados said. "It has been said that a high-born wench such as yourself scorns to utter falsehood. Let us see if that is correct."

She made no reply, and the face of Barbados grew purple with wrath. He closed and unclosed his great hands as though he would have liked to strangle her.

"Is Señor Zorro aboard?" he demanded again.

"Have you seen him?" she wanted to know.

"I have not. But I have seen some things that I imagine are his doing."

"And I notice that you and your lieutenant bear his mark," she said.

"Ha! Let me but get my hands on him, and he'll bear more than a mark!" Barbados declared. "I am having a search made of the ship. If he is found you'll see how a man can be sent to his death speedily."

The *señorita* gave a little cry and recoiled, her hands at her breast.

"Ha! You show fear for him!" Barbados cried. "So he is aboard, is he?"

"Have I said so?" she asked.

"You have not—but now you are going to tell me the truth. Wench, I'm done with trifling. You presume too much on the knowledge that you are to be the prize of an important man. Do you not know you are in my power? Could I not do with you as I pleased, and then heave you overboard, and tell this important gentleman later that you got the chance and threw yourself into the sea?"

Evil glistened suddenly in his eyes, and the little *señorita* recoiled again. Sanchez, who had remained standing near, laughed like a fiend.

"We could gamble for her," Sanchez suggested.

"This is my affair, and you will do well to remain silent," Barbados declared, whirling upon him.

Once more he faced Señorita Lolita, and the fiendish look upon his face made her flinch.

"Tell me all you know about this Señor Zorro!" Barbados commanded. "Did you slay the man in your cabin, or did this Señor Zorro do it? Answer me, wench! Reply here and now, else I teach you a lesson you will remember to your last hour."

He sprang forward suddenly and grasped her arm cruelly, and she cried out because of the indignity and the pain.

Señor Zorro, from his place of watching, flinched as though he had experienced the indignity and pain himself. He wanted to hurl himself forward and to the attack, but he realized that it would not last for long. He could not hope to engage the entire ship's company, though he made a long and running fight of it, and emerge from the combat the victor.

But there came an interruption. From forward was a hail:

"A sail! A sail!"

The pirates sprang to their feet. Those who had been sprawled upon the deck asleep awoke.

Barbados forgot the *señorita* for a moment and turned to look.

Behind, and bearing down upon them swiftly, came another ship. Señor Zorro knew, as did the pirates, that she had put out from the land before the dawn and far to the south of where the pirate ship had been at anchor.

Hope beat suddenly in Zorro's breast. She was a trading schooner, he could tell even at that distance. If only she carried Audre Ruiz and his friends! It was a question what would happen. If she was some honest vessel, perhaps she would fall victim to the pirate craft. She might not be prepared to fight.

Barbados issued a volley of commands. The pirate craft turned for a run farther out to sea, so that she could tack back and catch the oncoming ship between her and the shore.

Lookouts were posted to watch carefully. Sanchez ran here and there, echoing the orders of his chief.

From his hiding place Señor Zorro watched now the approaching vessel, and now the deck where Señorita Lolita was standing against the mast, forgotten for the moment.

Were he quite sure that ship carried his friends Señor Zorro could go into action. For he flattered himself that he would be able to hold his own until the other ship came up.

It appeared that the other vessel had no intention of running up the coast. She changed her course also, and bore after the pirate craft.

Señor Zorro watched her carefully. He could not make out her flag. At the distance he could see nothing except that she was of the type of trading schooner, and that she had swift heels. For she was gaining rapidly, as though sailed by experts. And the pirate craft was foul of bottom, needing careening and scraping.

Barbados had hurried to the rail and was watching the oncoming ship. Señorita Lolita saw it also, but did not seem to realize that it meant hope.

Perhaps she feared that the ship was but coming into grave danger, running into a conflict that would mean capture and death for her crew.

Señor Zorro glanced at the deck, and then back at the approaching vessel again. He saw that another sail was being sent aloft. It was broken out, snapped into place, the lines tautened. And Señor Zorro with difficulty restrained a cheer. On the white expanse of the sail, painted there in haphazard fashion, but easily made out, was a monster Z.

So his friends were on that ship! Señor Zorro felt better now. He glanced once more toward the deck, and realized that Barbados had seen what was on the sail also. For the pirate chief left the rail and stamped back to the *señorita's* side, determination in his manner and rage in his countenance.

"Now you'll speak the truth, wench!" he shouted. "Is Señor Zorro aboard this ship? If those are his friends coming up, then will we attend to him before we attend to them!"

"I do not care to hold conversation with you," she said.

"No? By my naked blade, I am in command here!" he roared. "An answer I intend to have."

He lurched forward and grasped her by the shoulders, shook her as a terrier shakes a rat, held her at arm's length and shook her again. She fought against crying out, but could not win the battle against such cruel odds.

One plaintive little cry drifted across the deck and straight into the heart of Señor Zorro.

He transferred his sword from his right hand to his left. He whipped the dagger from his belt and hurled it. His aim was poor, yet he had come close enough. The dagger was driven, quivering, into the mast between Barbados and the *señorita*.

Barbados, with a cry, sprang backward, and the *señorita* slumped to the deck at the foot of the mast. And Señor Zorro realized in that instant that he had stepped forward too far and had been seen. Sanchez gave a cry and started toward him. The pirates whirled from the rail to look. Barbados saw him.

"'Tis Señor Zorro!" Barbados shrieked. "After him! Fetch him to me alive! An extra share of loot to the man who gets him!"

It was the promise of loot that drove them on. They shrieked and rushed forward. Señor Zorro put the blade of his sword between his teeth and darted up into the rigging.

And then began a fight the like of which the pirates never had seen before. Señor Zorro seemed scarcely human. Up the rigging he went like a monkey. He sprang from spar to spar. Down the ratlines he rushed, down the ropes he slid.

Now and then he clashed with one of the pirates, and always the sword of Zorro darted in and out, and a wounded man was left behind.

"Seize him!" Barbados shrieked. "After him, dogs! Is one man to hold you off forever? Do not slay him! An extra share of loot—"

Señor Zorro struck the deck and darted across it. Sanchez retreated before his darting blade. He pierced the breast of a pirate who stepped before him, hurled another aside, sprang to the mast, and recovered his dagger. He stooped for an instant, and pressed the lips of the *señorita* to his own, and dashed on.

Now he was cornered, and now he fought his way to freedom. A dagger whirled past his head and buried itself in the deck beyond. Into the rigging he went again, up the ratlines, out along a spar.

They followed him, and he put his sword into its scabbard and sprang. Far below he caught another spar, ran to the mast, started downward again. One glance he gave at the approaching ship. His friends were gaining, but they still were far away.

Again they had him cornered, and again he escaped them by jumping to the deck below. He dashed around the deck cabin, met and defeated another man with a single clash of blades, and was at the rail.

There was grave danger on the deck, he knew, and so he went aloft once more. Up and up he went, while Barbados and Sanchez shrieked to the others to follow and get him.

"Alive! I want him alive!" Barbados screeched.

Another spring from spar to spar. Señor Zorro almost missed because of the rolling of the ship. But he caught and clung on, and scrambled to a place of safety. In toward the mast he hurried.

But there was a treacherous spot on the spar, where the mist had struck and clung, a wet spot made to cause a boot to slip. Señor Zorro felt himself reeling suddenly to one side. He grasped wildly—grasped nothing but empty air. His heart seemed to stop beating for an instant. He felt himself falling through space. To his ears came the terrified cry of the little *señorita*. The deck rushed up to meet him. He struck it with a crash and the darkness came.

Señorita Lolita gave another little cry and covered her face with her hands. Barbados and Sanchez rushed forward, the others at their heels.

Señor Zorro was unconscious for the moment, though the fall had broken no bones.

"Bind him!" Barbados cried, glancing back at the oncoming ship. "We attend to him first, and then to his friends. Water his head well and bring him back to life. Get ready a plank!"

The pirates rushed to do his bidding.

Señor Zorro's wrists were lashed behind his back. One man hurled water into his face, and he groaned and opened his eyes, and tried to sit up on the deck.

"Ha!" Barbados cried. "So it is Señor Zorro, eh? And now we can repay you for this little mark you put on my forehead, *señor*! Barbados, also, knows how to make payment!"

He gave a signal, and the pirates forced Zorro to his feet. He tried to fight, but they overpowered him. They braced him against the mast, while the *señorita* crept aside and watched.

"Hold the wench!" Barbados commanded two of the men. "We don't want her throwing herself overboard. And I wish her to witness what is to come."

The two men held her. Señor Zorro, half throttled, was kept against the mast. Barbados made another sign, and some of the men carried forward a heavy bar of iron and lashed it to Señor Zorro's wrists.

"To the rail with him!" Barbados commanded.

They forced him to the rail, and the two men urged the *señorita* along beside him. Over the rail a long, wide plank had been extended.

Señor Zorro knew what they meant to do to him. And now Señorita Lolita realized it, too.

"No, no!" she shrieked. "You must not do this thing!"

"Ha! Revenge is sweet!" Barbados cried. "Señor Zorro, you are about to descend to a watery hell! We'll let you take your sword with you, since you may need it fighting demons. You take the plunge, and then, when yon ship comes up, we attend to your friends! As for the *señorita*, know that she will be delivered safely to one who has bargained for her."

"Why not give me a chance in a fair fight?" Zorro asked. "Any two of you—any three—"

"Your friends are coming up, and we must prepare for them," Barbados replied, laughing. "You have fought your last fight on earth, *señor*. See if you can mark the brow of the devil with your cursed Z."

"Diego!" the *señorita* moaned.

"As a special favor you may kiss the wench," Barbados said. "It will be practice for her. And take with you to the bottom of the sea the knowledge that another will kiss her soon."

The *señorita* rushed forward and threw her arms around him and kissed him, unashamed.

"Diego! I'll follow you!" she said.

"'Tis a merry end," Señor Zorro declared. "Be brave of heart! Our friends are at hand, *señorita*! If Don Audre Ruiz is aboard that ship he will know how to save you—and how to avenge me."

Again they kissed, and then the two pirates jerked her roughly backward.

Barbados laughed like a fiend.

"Practice for the other man!" he roared. "When Captain Ramón—"

"So it is Ramón?" Zorro cried.

"*Sí!* And a lot of good the knowledge will do you now."

"This much good—that I shall not die!" Zorro answered.

"If you do not, then indeed are you a man! With a weight on your lashed wrists— Enough!" he exclaimed. "Put him on the plank!"

They lifted him and stood him upon it, facing him toward the sea. They forced him a short distance from the rail.

"Diego!" the *señorita* cried, agony in her voice.

At her cry the plank was tipped.

And with her cry ringing in his ears Señor Zorro shot downward like a man of metal—shot downward into the tossing sea, and was gone!

PART THREE

PART III

TWELVE
TO THE RESCUE

UPON THE FRANTIC departure of Don Diego Vega from Reina de Los Angeles, Don Audre Ruiz took command of the situation and the *caballeros* simultaneously. There was none willing to dispute his leadership. Don Audre always had been a leader when there was an enterprise that called for hard riding and hard fighting in the bright face of danger.

Captain Ramón was not to be found, and Sergeant Gonzales had ridden away with the soldiers. So Don Audre noised it abroad that he and his friends intended pursuing the pirates as speedily as possible, and made a quick search for mounts.

They acquired enough, presently, but the horses were a sorry lot when compared to the *caballeros's* own, which the pirates had stolen. And without changing their attire, retaining the splendid costumes they had been wearing at Don Diego's bachelor feast and with their jeweled swords at their sides, they rode up the slope and took the trail that would carry them to the sea.

Don Audre decided against following the pirates' tracks. He knew that they would reach the coast long before the *caballeros*, and would embark. Don Diego would do what he could, which would be little. And Don Audre realized that their only hope was to get to the trading schooner, put out in it, and make an attempt to overtake Barbados and his evil crew.

They rode with what speed they could, shouting at their poor mounts and at one another, along the slopes, down the dusty trails and so toward the distant sea. They crossed the trail of the pirates who had looted the Pulido *hacienda*, but ignored it. Don Audre Ruiz knew where the trading schooner would be anchored, some miles to the south of where the pirate ship undoubtedly had touched, and that place was his objective.

Hour after hour they rode, urging their jaded horses to their utmost, glad that the moon was bright and that they could make as good progress as in the day. And, when they finally were within a couple of miles of the sea, and also an hour of the dawn, Don Audre suddenly raised his hand and reined in his horse, and those behind stopped with him. A native was standing in the middle of the trail.

Don Audre approached him slowly, hand on the hilt of his dagger. There were some natives who were not to be trusted. But when he drew near he recognized the fellow as one who had worked at his father's *hacienda*.

"What do you here?" Don Audre demanded.

"I saw the *señor* coming from the distance with his friends," the native answered. "I have news."

"Speak!"

"I was coming across the hills, *señor*, and saw the pirates."

"Ha! Talk quickly!" Audre Ruiz commanded.

"I went into hiding, lest they slay me. They had good horses and much loot, also a girl—"

"Tell us of that!"

"It was the *señorita* Don Diego Vega expects to wed," the native said. "They took her with them to the shore, and presently more pirates came from Reina de Los Angeles. They went aboard their ship, taking the *señorita* and the loot with them."

"What else?"

"There was a man appeared, *señor*, and killed one of the pirates. I got a glimpse of him, Don Audre, and it was Señor Zorro, the one that—"

"Ha! Zorro!" Audre shrieked. "Speak quickly!"

"He ran from them, and they gave up the pursuit. But when the boats started from the land, he dived into the sea and swam after them. And he did not return!"

"Then is he aboard the pirate craft!" Don Audre declared.

"The pirate ship sailed to the south, *señor*."

"Good!" Audre cried. "Know you anything of the trading schooner?"

"*Sí, señor!* She is anchored straight ahead, and the men expect to start for Reina de Los Angeles in the morning to trade."

"They will not, though they do not know it." Don Audre said. "Here is gold for you, fellow. Ha! So the pirate ship sailed to the south. That means that the rogues are going to their hidden rendezvous somewhere down the coast. We'll get the trading schooner and pursue! Forward!"

But, as they would have started, Don Audre Ruiz raised a hand and stopped them again. From the rear had come the beating of a horse's hoofs. Don Audre motioned to the *caballeros*, and they scattered to either side of the road and prepared to receive the newcomer.

Nearer grew the beating of hoofs, and a horseman appeared, riding frantically through the moonlight down the slope and toward them. When he saw them, he reined up, and stopped in their midst in a shower of gravel and sand and dust. The reckless rider was Sergeant Gonzales.

"Ha, *señores*!" he called. "I have overtaken you finally, it appears."

"And to what end?" Don Audre Ruiz asked, urging his horse forward and glaring at the soldier. "You have news?"

"Not so, *señor*! I come in search of it. I returned to Reina de Los Angeles with my troopers to learn of the pirates and what they had done. I learned, also, of your departure, so left my men and rode after you. Captain Ramón was not at the *presidio*. As the next soldier of rank—"

"It is in our minds to get the trading schooner and give pursuit," Ruiz told him.

"That is a worthy idea!" Sergeant Gonzales declared. "Too long have these bloody pirates infested our shores. Meal mush and goat's milk! Let us go forward!"

"Are you seeking to take command of this expedition?" Don Audre Ruiz demanded, hotly. "This is a private rescue party of *caballeros*, I would have you know, and not a detachment of the Governor's men! We have small love for the Governor!"

"Though I wear his uniform, I say the same thing," Sergeant Gonzales declared. "But I am after pirates! I care not who commands, so that I get a chance at a pirate with my trusty blade! Ha! When I meet a pirate face to face—"

"Spare us your boasting!" Don Audre said.

"Boasting?" shrieked the sergeant. "Boasting? Perchance you would like to cross blades with me in answer to that insult?"

"You are safe in making the challenge, knowing that I would not stoop to do so," Don Audre said.

"And you are safe in refusing, having the ability to hide behind your gentle blood!" the sergeant returned.

"*Señor*—"

Sergeant Gonzales urged his mount closer to that of Don Audre, but the expression in the sergeant's face had changed peculiarly, and his countenance did not show rage.

"*Señor*, it is true," Sergeant Gonzales observed, "that I am but a poor soldier without blue blood in my veins. My father was a butcher and my mother's father raised swine. But Don Diego Vega has been good enough to term himself my friend. And now that he is in peril, I ride with his other friends to his rescue, and the rescue of his lady! I trust the señor will not misunderstand! I do not seek to equal my betters. If I am not good enough to ride with you, *caballero*, then I ride by myself! But I ride!"

Don Audre Ruiz bent forward and searched the sergeant's face by the light of the one torch the company had burning. Then he extended his hand.

"Sergeant Gonzales, it is for me to ask your pardon," Don Audre said, grandly. "I would not be worthy the blood in my veins did I do less. Any friend of Don Diego Vega is welcome on this expedition. But, have you leave of absence?"

"Ha! I took it!" Sergeant Gonzales roared, grinning broadly. "Captain Ramón was not at the *presidio*. Being the next in rank, I ordered myself to set out on the trail and get a full report of the occurrence. When I am able to make that report I return."

"Ride you with us!" Don Audre said. "Thus we have the sanction of the soldiery and official approval of our deeds."

"I shall approve anything that has to do with causing the death of pirates!" Sergeant Gonzales declared.

The moon disappeared entirely, and the night was dark. They rode forward slowly now, careful not to get off the trail, but they did not have much farther to go. Soon they came to the crest of a hill, and below them they heard the hissing sea, and saw the lights of a ship riding at anchor a short distance from the shore.

Down to the surf they urged their mounts. And there they met with another surprise. For a horseman was awaiting them there in the darkness. Don Audre Ruiz gasped in astonishment when he recognized old Fray Felipe.

"We left you in the town, *fray*!" he said. "And how is it that we now find you here? Is this some sort of a miracle?"

"I departed the town while you were yet searching for horses," Fray Felipe explained. "I got a mount for myself and came ahead, because I cannot ride like the wind, as do you young *caballeros*. It was in my mind that you would make for the trading schooner. I heard you say as much."

"But why have you come?" Don Audre wanted to know.

"I have known Don Diego Vega and the little *señorita* since they were babes in arms, and I was to have married them to-day," the old *fray* replied.

"But fighting is not your forte!" Don Audre declared. "You are old, and you wear a gown. Do you remain behind and pray for our success, and let us wield the blades! That were better, *fray*."

"I am willing to make my prayers. But I have taken a vow," Fray Felipe replied. "I must return the golden goblet the pirates stole from the church."

"Then you would go with us?" Don Audre asked.

"*Sí!* I already have communicated with the captain of the trading schooner, *señor*. He is coming ashore now in one of his boats. Thus time will be saved."

THIRTEEN
TRAGEDY AT A DISTANCE

THE *CABALLEROS* DISMOUNTED stiffly and gathered near the water line. In from the distant trading schooner a boat was coming, driven over the choppy water by silent oarsmen. Half a dozen men were in her, and their flaring torches touched the sea with streaks of flame. They approached the shore carefully, and on guard, as though fearing some trap set by thieves, and by the light of the torches those on the land could see that the men in the boat were heavily armed.

Don Audre Ruiz and Fray Felipe went forward and met the boat at the water's edge and greeted the schooner's captain as he stepped to land. He was a regular trader who carried goods overland from the sea to Reina de Los Angeles every now and then. He traveled as far as San Diego de Alcála to the south, and as far as San Francisco de Asis to the north—a bold fellow and honest, well and favorably known.

"What is all this tumult?" the captain demanded. "Fray Felipe, are you not? Ha! I thought that I recognized you, good *fray*! And Don Audre Ruiz, whose father has purchased much goods of me. Sundry *caballeros* and men of rank, also! In what way may I be of service to you, *señores*? Have you ridden out all this long way in the night to have first choice of my stock of goods?"

Don Audre Ruiz told him swiftly. "We want your ship, to pursue a pirate craft!" he said.

"How is this, *señor*?" the captain cried. "There are pirates in these waters?"

"*Sí!* And possibly within half a dozen miles of you," Don Audre told him. "Early in the night they raided Reina de Los Angeles. They also raided the

Pulido *hacienda,* and carried away the *señorita,* who was to have wed Don Diego Vega this day."

"By the saints!" the schooner's captain swore. "They stole the bride-to-be of Señor Zorro? Is he here with you?"

"He followed them, going ahead of us, and possibly managed to get aboard their ship," Don Audre explained. "The pirate craft has sailed by this time. They went toward the south. They will beat out to sea for a distance. If we can start soon it may be possible to overhaul them."

"How many rascals in the pirate crew?" the captain of the schooner asked.

"Not more than threescore, as nearly as we can judge," Don Audre replied. "And here are a score of *caballeros,* and we are ready to fight!"

The captain of the schooner drew a deep breath, held it for an instant, and then expelled it with great force. And during this process he evidently made up his mind concerning the matter.

"*Señores,* I am yours to command!" he said. "My ship is yours, and her crew. If I can do anything to help rid the seas of such vermin, I am more than willing. My schooner is a swift vessel in light winds such as we find now. I'll signal the other boats and have you aboard as soon as is possible."

"You will not fail to profit by it," Don Audre Ruiz told him.

"I am not doing it with the expectation of profit," the captain declared. "I detest thieves, and I admire honest men! I have many friends in Reina de Los Angeles, some of whom probably have suffered at the hands of these pirates. And, above all, I did admire the exploits of this Señor Zorro, as Don Diego was called. It will be a pleasure, *señores,* to aid you in this."

He called to his men, and they signaled to the ship with their torches. Out of the darkness and across the tumbling sea came more boats from the schooner. The *caballeros* turned their horses adrift, knowing that they would be picked up and returned, made certain that they had daggers and swords handy, and got quickly into the boats and put out to the ship.

Sergeant Gonzales and Fray Felipe, by accident, were placed in the same craft, sitting side by side on one of the wide thwarts. Sergeant Gonzales observed the *fray* carefully from the corners of his eyes. The sergeant wished to talk, having kept silent for some minutes, and the *fray* was the nearest man he knew.

"Never did I think to join hands with you in an enterprise, *fray*!" the sergeant said, puffing out his cheeks. "If I am not badly mistaken, you are the gowned one who stopped me in the plaza on a certain occasion, and made remarks about soldiers drinking too much wine at the *posada*. Ha! But pirates' raids cause rescue parties, and rescue parties cause strange comrades!"

"I am appreciating the fact," Fray Felipe replied quietly and with a smile.

"So they stole your sacred goblet, did they?" Sergeant Gonzales said smoothly. "*Fray*, when I have rescued the *señorita*, aided Don Diego to escape, and annihilated the pirates with my blade, then will I regain your goblet for you! Steal church goblets and brides, eh? Ha! Meal mush and goat's milk!"

"If your sword arm is half as strong as your tongue, *señor*," Fray Felipe rebuked him gently, "then the pirates are as good as dead already!"

Sergeant Gonzales whirled upon him.

"Ha! Stinging words from a gentle *fray*!" he gasped. "Is it possible for me to get insulted where and when I can wipe out the insult with a thrust? A *caballero* insults me and then refuses to fight because of the noble blood in his veins and the poor swill in mine! A *fray* insults me—and I cannot fight a man who wears a gown! Meal mush and goat's milk! But wait until we meet up with these pirates! Let a pirate but insult me, and—ha! My blade shall be bathed in blood!"

Sergeant Gonzales turned away abruptly to nurse his wrath, and Fray Felipe smiled and his eyes twinkled. He waited a moment, then touched the sergeant on the shoulder.

"Soldiers and *frailes* alike are needed in the world," Fray Felipe said. "There are times when a hardy soldier should be gentle—and even there are times when a *fray* should fight. Let us be friends!"

"*Fray*," Sergeant Gonzales declared, "you are a noble fellow, after all! I forgive you for what you said about drinking wine. When the muss commences, *fray*, get you behind me. My sword shall shield you, *fray*!"

"I thank you," Fray Felipe said. "And I shall shield you in turn with my prayers."

"Prayers may have power," Sergeant Gonzales told him, "but when it comes to fighting pirates give me my trusty blade! *Fray*, a pirate has not sense enough to know when a prayer is directed against him!"

Soon they came alongside the schooner and mounted to the deck by the light of torches. The boats were swung aboard, and the captain and Don Audre Ruiz held a long conference. Then there came a volley of orders, the anchor came up and the sails filled, and the schooner crept off the shore and away from the land through the black night.

Straight out to sea they went, gathering headway, and in time a faint streak of light showed across the land and the dawn came. *Caballeros* and crew strained their eyes and swept the sea in every direction. And finally the sharp eyes of one of the men aloft discovered a sail.

The course of the trading schooner was changed, and the chase began. Nearer their quarry they crept as the sun came up and bathed the sea and the land, glistening through the haze. Glasses were leveled at the distant craft.

"She is the pirate!" the schooner's captain declared. "Her flag of iniquity flies from her mast!"

He bellowed another volley of orders to his crew, and they crowded on all sail. They rushed about the schooner, preparing her for the battle. The eager *caballeros* looked to their blades, the crew to their cutlasses.

"If Zorro is aboard that craft he should know that his friends are near at hand for the rescue," Don Audre said.

And then it was that they got out a sail and painted a gigantic Z upon it, and sent it aloft. It was their banner of battle, a flag of war that betokened their allegiance to a man and a cause.

"Courage and swift work does it!" the schooner's captain told Don Audre. "We are greatly outnumbered. But my crew has had dealings with pirates before, hence each man will fight with the strength of five. And you and your friends, Don Audre, have good reason for fighting like fiends."

"We are prepared to do it," Don Audre replied. "Think you that we can overhaul the pirate?"

"It is but a question of time," the captain declared. "The pirate sails prettily, but her bottom is foul. I can tell that much at this distance. Pirates are too lazy to keep a ship in perfect shape. And this little schooner of mine is a swift craft and in prime condition."

They gained steadily, and meanwhile they watched the distant pirate ship continually. They saw that there was some sort of a tumult on board. Don Audre Ruiz, standing at the rail near the bow, with a glass glued to his eye, watched carefully.

"It is probable that Señor Zorro is fighting the entire pirate company," he announced. "I can see men running about the rigging. Let us pray that we may be in time."

Sergeant Gonzales, standing near him, uttered an oath that the presence of Fray Felipe did not keep back.

"Meal mush and goat's milk!" he exclaimed. "Let us crowd on more sail and have at these pirates!" He swept his blade from its scabbard. "That for a pirate!" he shrieked, thrusting about him in a rage. "This for a pirate! Ha!"

"Save your breath and your strength," Don Audre advised him. "You may have need of them both soon."

"Did you hear that, *fray*?" Sergeant Gonzales demanded, whirling upon old Felipe. "More insults, and I cannot avenge them! A *caballero* insults me and will not fight, and I cannot fight a *fray*! By the time we clash with these pirates I shall be in a fine rage, and work it off on their worthless bodies. Ha!"

Don Audre Ruiz gave a gasp and called some of the *caballeros* to his side.

"Look!" he directed. "They are making some poor devil walk the plank! By the saints, 'tis Zorro!"

"Zorro!" the others cried.

"Look! And the little *señorita* is standing at the rail, forced to watch!"

There was a moment of horrified silence. The face of Don Audre Ruiz was white as he contemplated the fate of his friend. The *caballeros* said not a word, but those who had glasses watched, and the others strained their eyes in an effort to see.

And then Don Audre Ruiz gave a low cry of horror and turned quickly away, as though he could endure the sight no longer.

What he had seen had been enough. There were traces of tears in his eyes, and his voice choked.

"He is gone!" Don Audre said. "Don Diego, my friend! We can only avenge him now!"

"Gone!" Sergeant Gonzales cried, sudden tears in his eyes, too. He brushed them away roughly and blinked. "Don Diego gone? Then, by the saints, will my blade be thrust as it never has been thrust before! Now, by the saints—"

His vow ended in a choke of emotion, and he turned quickly away. Don Audre, his eyes stinging, his lips set in a thin, straight line, turned to Fray Felipe.

"Say your prayers for him," he directed. "And pray, also, that we will know how to avenge him when we come alongside! *Dios!* Give strength to my arm!"

FOURTEEN
OUT OF THE DEPTHS

SMILING in the face of death, Señor Zorro yet battled to keep from showing his genuine emotions, because of the presence of the *señorita*. But in that awful moment when he stood upon the plank, looking first at the evil faces of Barbados and Sanchez, and then at the agonized countenance of Señorita Lolita Pulido, he knew what torture meant.

It was not that Señor Zorro was afraid of death in itself—a thing that must come to every human being in the end. But his agony came from a knowledge of what he would leave behind when he took the plunge into the sea.

The woman he had hoped to make his bride, his friends, his father, his estate—he was leaving them all for the Great Unknown. And he was young, and had not lived his fill of life. Besides, he was leaving the *señorita* in grave danger. He could only hope that his friends in the vessel behind would be able to be of service to her, and that they would know how to avenge him.

Barbados gave his last mocking laugh, and Señor Zorro felt the plank tipping. He felt himself losing his balance. The heavy weight on his wrists was almost bending him backward. He knew how swiftly it would carry him down into the depths of the sea. Then would come a brief and useless struggle, he supposed, a moment of horror—and the end!

His eyes met those of the *señorita* yet again. And then it seemed that everything gave way beneath him and he shot downward.

There came a splash of water as he struck the surface—he felt its sudden chill—and then the waves closed over his head. He was a famous swimmer, but no man can swim with a heavy bar of metal tied to his wrists, and those wrists lashed behind his back.

Mechanically Señor Zorro protected himself as he struck the water, as though for a deep dive. He drew air into his lungs until it seemed that they would burst. He kicked in vain against the down-pulling power of the heavy weight. Down and down he went into the depths until the light from the surface faded and he found himself in darkness.

Señor Zorro prayed and worked at the same instant. He jerked his wrists from side to side behind his back, trying to force them apart. He expelled a tiny bit of air now and then as he descended, but retained it as much as possible.

Often he had played at remaining as long as possible beneath water, but it is one thing to do so when a man has the knowledge that he can spring to the surface at any time, and quite another when he has reason to believe that he never will reach the surface again at all.

Yet he continued to struggle as he shot downward. Red flashes were before his eyes now, and a multitude of faces and scenes seemed to flit before him.

In that awful instant he relived half his life.

"*Dios!*" he thought. "If this be death—"

Another tug he gave at his wrists. The man who had lashed the heavy weight there had not done his work well. Perhaps he was too busy watching Barbados and fearing him. Perhaps he had held a sneaking admiration for this Señor Zorro, who had offered battle to an entire ship's company. However, the rope that held the weight gave a trifle.

Señor Zorro, in his agony, realized that. He tugged again, and then pressed his palms close together and drew in his wrists as much as possible. The heavy weight, dragging downward, pulled the loose loop over the wrists and hands. Zorro felt an immediate relief. He realized what had happened. And then he began his battle to reach the surface. The weight was gone, but his wrists were still lashed together behind his back.

He kicked and struggled and shot upward. He expelled more of the precious air his lungs retained. His chest was burning, his ears were ringing, he was almost unconscious because of the pressure of the water he had been forced to endure.

He saw a glimmer of light, but knew that the surface was yet far away. And it occurred to him that even the surface did not mean life. For his wrists were yet bound behind him, and he was miles from the shore.

On he went, up and up, struggling and fighting. He jerked at his wrists until they were raw and bleeding, but to no avail. Those who had lashed his wrists had done better than the one who had fastened the weight to them.

And finally he gave a last struggle, a last kick, and felt the blessed air striking upon his face.

He fought to get into the proper position for resting as much as he could. He kept afloat, and he drew in great gasps of air, and finally reduced his breathing to normal. And then, as he rose on the crest of a wave, he looked around as well as he could.

The pirate ship was some distance away, sailing slowly before a gentle breeze. Señor Zorro found himself floating in her wake. He could see men rushing around her deck and up into her rigging, but at the distance could not guess their tasks.

The wave dropped him and lifted him again, spinning him halfway around. Señor Zorro gasped at the risk of swallowing a portion of salt water. Bearing down upon him was the other craft, the one with the gigantic Z up on the sail. Zorro saw that he was directly in her path.

Not much hope burned in his breast, yet the spirit of combat still lived. He would not give up so long as there was the slightest chance. He would fight—fight—until, exhausted, he sank for the last time toward the bottom of the sea.

Those on the approaching ship did not see him, for they were watching the pirate craft and preparing for the battle that was to come.

He hailed those on board, but his voice was drowned by the roar of the water against the schooner's bows. He saw that she would strike him, and kicked frantically to work himself to one side of the track she was following. Another glance ahead at the pirate craft convinced him that the schooner would not change her course.

Once more he tugged at his bonds, to no avail. He felt himself drawn in toward the schooner's bows, and fought against the pull of the water helplessly. He was picked up, hurled forward, whirled around. Had he saved himself from the depths, he wondered, to be crushed senseless by the bow of the craft that carried his friends? Then she was upon him. He rose with the crest of a wave and was hurled at the bow.

He saw an anchor chain that was loosely looped and a dragging line. If he could but catch one of those and make his way to the deck, there might be some chance. Once more the sea whirled him and cast him forward. He came against the swinging loop of anchor chain with a crash, grasped it, was lifted and dropped, but held on!

For a moment he rested, panting, realizing how precarious was his position. He threw one leg around the swinging chain. How to reach the bowsprit he could not fathom. Those above would pay no attention to him, and could not hear him if he hailed. And to climb that swinging loop of chain would be a task for an athlete with his hands unbound.

The bow of the ship dipped, and Señor Zorro felt himself soused beneath the water for an instant. He gripped the chain with his hands and his leg and fought to maintain his position. His arms were aching, and the chain had cut through his clothing already and was chafing at his leg. Once more the bow dipped, and Zorro slipped a few feet along the chain, unable to stop his descent.

He gripped with his leg again. His hands came to a stop, and he realized that the rope that bound them had found an obstruction. Zorro worked slowly and carefully with his fingers, even as he held on. One of the links of the chain, he found, was imperfect, had cracked, and presented on one side a jagged edge.

Hope sang in his breast once more. But he knew that he would have to work carefully. He did not dare release his hold entirely, for a sudden dip of the bow and the quick wash of the water would be enough to sweep him from the chain. But he sawed back and forth as well as he could, pulling the rope across the rough edge of the chain link.

He glanced ahead. The ships were not far apart now, and the schooner swung a bit to starboard, so as to bear down upon the pirate craft from a more advantageous angle. Zorro worked frantically, and after a time he felt the rope give. His wrists were raw and paining. His leg was bleeding already. There were pains in his head, and his vision was imperfect, but hope sang within him once more.

He sawed and sawed, and once more he glanced ahead. It would not be long now before the ships clashed. He wanted to be up on the deck, normal breath in his nostrils and the sword of Zorro in his hand, to aid his friends, to fight his way to the deck of the pirate craft and to the *señorita's* side.

The rope gave again. Señor Zorro was forced to rest for a moment, leaning back on the chain. A wave swept him to one side, and he thought for an instant that he was gone. But he regained his balance and continued his sawing.

And presently he knew that he was free. The rope dangled from one wrist only. He gave an exclamation of delight and thanks, gripped the chain, and turned over. He regarded his bleeding wrists, hesitated a moment, gathered breath and courage, and commenced the perilous ascent of the chain.

It was a painful and difficult task. Señor Zorro set his teeth into his lower lip and struggled upward foot by foot. The swinging chain, slippery, from the sea, threatened to pitch him back into the water. Every few feet he was obliged to stop, to gasp for breath and close his eyes for a moment because the pain in his wrists and leg made him weak with nausea.

He came within a short distance of the vessel, slipped back, and forced his way upward again. And finally he grasped with one hand the chain port and held on. His hope had increased now. Nothing would make him loose his hold, he told himself.

A moment he rested, then forced his way upward again. The schooner was very close to the pirate ship now. On the deck above him Señor Zorro could hear Don Audre Ruiz shrieking instructions to the *caballeros* and the captain shouting to his crew.

He managed to get up to the butt of the bowsprit, and there, safe from the sea, he rested for a moment again. The two ships would crash together in a minute or so, he saw. He raised his head weakly, and took a deep breath, and then struggled to his feet, ready to spring down to the deck.

His hand went down to whip the sword of Zorro from its scabbard. The schooner yawed suddenly as her helmsman fought to get a position of advantage. The big jib swung back, whipped by the angry wind.

Señor Zorro was looking down at the deck, and he did not see his danger. Don Audre Ruiz turned at the instant, shrieked, and rubbed his eyes.

"Zorro!" he cried.

He was seen from the deck of the pirate craft, too.

Barbados and Sanchez caught sight of him. Sanchez crossed himself quickly, and the face of Barbados turned white.

And then the jib cracked against Señor Zorro's body, knocked him from his precarious perch, and hurled him once more into the sea!

FIFTEEN
A SHOW OF GRATITUDE

THE SCHOONER SAILED ON, and came against the pirate ship with a crash. But here was a battle unlike the usual one when honest men met pirates. As a usual thing, the pirates could be expected to board and slay without mercy, to loot, and then either to destroy the ill-fated vessel or take it away a prize. And the honest men could be expected only to offer what defense they could. But here was a case where the honest men were more than willing to carry the fight to the pirates. For Don Audre Ruiz and his *caballero* friends had seen Señor Zorro walk the plank, and also they fought to rescue a lady.

But both forces found themselves disconcerted at the outset. Don Audre Ruiz, glancing toward the bow of the schooner, was sure that he saw Señor Zorro standing there against a background of sky and water, his figure dripping. He rubbed his eyes and looked again—and Señor Zorro was gone!

"'Tis the spirit of Zorro come to aid us!" Don Audre cried. "I saw him for a moment, waving his hand at me and reaching for his blade! The spirit of Zorro fights with us!"

The *caballeros* were not certain what he meant, but they cheered his words and rushed toward the rail, their gleaming blades ready to be dyed a crimson. Fray Felipe knelt beside the mast in prayer. But Sergeant Gonzales, standing with his feet wide apart and his sword in his hand, stared foolishly toward the bow and gasped his astonishment and fear.

"I saw him!" the sergeant shrieked. "I saw Don Diego, my friend! By the saints—"

The ships crashed together. But the pirates did not rush as was their custom. For fear had clutched at their superstitious natures, even as it had clutched at Barbados and Sanchez, his evil lieutenant. Sanchez had shrieked the news, but Barbados did not heed his intelligence. Barbados himself had seen Señor Zorro standing against the sky. And how may a man do that when he has been sent to the bottom of the sea with a heavy weight fastened to him?

"Fiends of hell!" Barbados screeched. "This Zorro must be a demon!"

"We cannot fight against ghosts!" Sanchez cried. "We are lost before we commence."

Barbados seemed to come to himself and shake off his terror in part. He instantly was eager to win free from the trading schooner. He did not fear the *caballeros,* who were greatly outnumbered now, but he did fear the supernatural. He forgot the chance for murder and loot, and wanted only to get away.

Barbados shrieked his commands, and the half-stupefied pirates ran to execute them. The pirate craft swung away from the schooner, so that men could not spring from one ship to the other. There were less than half a dozen clashes of blades; less than half a dozen minor wounds.

Slowly the pirate craft fell away. The helmsman of the schooner worked frantically to bring his ship back into the wind. The *caballeros* and the members of the schooner's crew waited, eager for the two ships to come together again, that they might engage the pirates and fight to victory.

Barbados howled more commands. From the pirate ship came a rain of fire balls, and flaming torches were hurled. It was a favorite pirate trick, and the men knew what their commander wanted. Clouds of pungent smoke rolled across the deck of the schooner.

The *caballeros* gasped and fought to get to the clean, pure air. Their nostrils and throats were raw, their eyes stinging.

Through the dense smoke they could see little. The pirate ship gradually was lengthening the distance between her and the trading schooner. The pirates' work had been done.

For the sails of the schooner were wrapped in flames, and bits of them fell, burning, to the deck below. Flames licked at the tarred rigging and spread out on the spars.

"She's making away!" Don Audre Ruiz cried. "She's running from us!"

There seemed to be no question about it now. The pirates were hurrying away without giving battle. And the raging *caballeros* wanted battle, and they remembered that the *señorita* was yet on the pirate craft.

The captain was howling to his crew, and the men were fighting the raging flames. The *caballeros,* forgetting their silks and satins and plumes, ran to help. Here was a foe more formidable than pirates of the open sea.

The schooner drifted with the water and the wind in the wake of the pirate ship. The smoke drifted away, and finally the fire was extinguished. Quick inventory was taken of the damage.

It did not amount to so very much, since the rigging had not been burned to a great extent. But the sails were gone, for the greater part, and pursuit for the moment at an end.

Again the captain shouted his commands, and as his men hurried to carry them out he turned to Don Audre.

"I have other sails, *señor*," he explained. "They will be in place as rapidly as my men can get them there. The craft of ill-omen cannot get far before we are upon her heels again. She is running out to sea once more. She would lose sight of us before she turns toward the accursed spot where they have their land rendezvous. Their behavior astounds me; they acted as if they had seen a ghost!"

"And so did I!" Don Audre declared. "I'll swear that, for an instant, I saw Señor Zorro standing at the butt of the bowsprit—and then he was gone!"

"By the saints, I saw him myself!" Sergeant Gonzales shouted. "He was here to aid us! Man or spirit, I know not—but he was here! And now he has disappeared!"

Fray Felipe came toward them. "It cannot be that he is alive and aboard," he told them, "else he would discover himself to us at once. Perhaps it was but a strong hope that caused you to imagine the sight."

"*Fray*, I swore friendship with you, but I'll break the compact if you say such a thing again!" Sergeant Gonzales declared. "I saw him, I say! Man or spirit, I know not—but I saw him!"

The *caballeros* were busy helping the crew with the new sails. One by one they were sheeted home, and presently the schooner gathered headway once more. On it sailed, in the wake of the pirate craft, vengeance only delayed.

Far behind, Señor Zorro watched her grow smaller and smaller, and the flare of hope that had been in his heart dwindled to a mere spark again.

His unexpected plunge into the sea before he had recovered from the first ordeal had unnerved him for the moment. He had come to the surface to find that the schooner had drifted away. Before he could handle himself to advantage she was at some distance, and the pirate craft was drawing away from the ship of smoke and flame.

There was a strong tide running, and Señor Zorro was too weak to fight against it. Near him there drifted a spar that had been torn away when the ships had crashed together. He struggled through the swirling water and managed to reach it, and drew himself upon it to sprawl there almost breathless, gasping, exhausted. He was too weak to signal his friends, and he doubted whether they would see him did he do so.

Shouting would be a waste of breath, he knew; and so, stretched across the spar, he fought to keep his consciousness, closing his eyes and forcing himself to breathe normally. When some strength had returned to him he sat upright and looked across the sea. The pirate craft was in the distance. The schooner, the fires extinguished, some of her sails in place, was drawing away from him rapidly. Señor Zorro gave thanks for that—his friends were not deserting the *señorita*.

He began to take stock of his predicament. Far away he could see a dirty streak on the horizon, and he knew it for the land he would have to reach.

He was in sore condition for the hazardous journey. His wrists were raw and bleeding; his leg pained him. He scarcely could see because of the glare of the sun on the water. Thirst tortured him; hunger added to the torture.

Señor Zorro sat up on the spar and smiled a sorry smile. He made sure that his blade still remained at his side.

"Sword of Zorro, we are in a sorry state!" he declared. "This is an emergency such as never have we faced before. But we must win through!"

A moment he hesitated, and then, as though to give courage to himself he raised his voice again, this time in his song:

"*Atención!* A *caballero's* near—"

But his voice broke, and he told himself that he was a fool to attempt to sing out there in the wild waste of waters, clinging to a spar. Far better to concern himself about getting to the land.

Señor Zorro rested a short time longer, watching the disappearing ships. And turning, he looked at the distant land.

"Sword of Zorro, we travel toward the east!" he announced. "If ever I touch dry land again, there I remain for some time to come. This seafaring is a sorry business!"

But he said that merely to amuse himself, of course. He would fare forth, to sea again at any time to rescue the Señorita Lolita, and well he knew it. He only hoped that Don Audre Ruiz and the others would be of service to her.

He adjusted himself as well as he could, and started to swim, clinging to the spar. That rendered his progress slow, but he did not dare cast it aside, for he knew that he never would reach the distant land. For a time he swam, and then he floated on the spar and rested, and then urged himself to swim again. On and on through the hours, while the sun traveled across the heavens, he forced the spar through the water.

It seemed to him that he was nearing the land, but he could not be sure.

There might be a treacherous current in these waters, against which he was expending his strength in vain. But he did not stop.

His mind was a maelstrom, his muscles acted mechanically. Now and then pains shot up his legs and along his back, and often he swam for minutes at a time with his eyes closed. He watched the sun begin its descent toward the sea, and yet he swam.

At times songs rang through his brain, at other times he caught himself mouthing meaningless phrases. And then he thought of the Señorita Lolita, and swam on.

Twilight came. The sun disappeared. There was a period of darkness, and then the surface of the sea was touched with the glory of the moon. Señor Zorro could not see the land now, but he knew in which direction it lay, and swam on, a few minutes at a time.

And thus passed the night. But before the dark space just before the dawn, Señor Zorro was laughing raucously, out of his wits. Some god of good fortune kept him swimming in the proper direction. And when the sun appeared again, it brought a new agony to his eyes, new tortures of thirst. He swallowed salt water and spat it out, and found that it had made him ill. For a time he was stretched across the spar, weak, sick, on the verge of delirium.

He fancied that a myriad of pirate vessels were about him, bearing down upon him. He saw the pretty, laughing face of the Señorita Lolita in the mist that hung above the sea. He laughed back at her, and once again his cracked voice rose in a song:

"*Atención!* A *caballero's* near—"

He felt himself grow suddenly weak. It seemed to him that the land was near at last, but he could not be sure. He drew himself upon the spar, sprawling across it.

"Must—rest—" Señor Zorro gasped.

And with the gasp he passed into unconsciousness.

Back to earth he struggled as through a land of hideous dreams. He tossed and groaned and tried to open his eyes, but felt that he could not. There seemed to be a roaring in his ears that was not of the sea. And finally it came to him that it was a human voice, attempting to beat through his unconsciousness and bring him to an understanding of things.

"*Señor! Señor—*" the voice said.

Señor Zorro struggled yet again, groaned once more, and opened his eyes. But not into the burning glare of the open sea! He was in cool shade, he found, and from a distance came the hissing of the surf. He blinked his eyes rapidly, felt something at his lips, and drank deeply of pure, cold water.

"*Señor!*" There was the voice again. "For the love of the saints, *señor*, come back to life!"

Full consciousness returned to him in a breath. He opened his eyes wider and struggled to sit up. Then he saw that he was in some sort of a poor hut, and that a native was beside him, with an arm beneath his shoulders.

"Ha!" Señor Zorro gasped.

"Thank the saints, *señor*!" the native cried.

Señor Zorro, with the help of the native, sat up. He had been stretched on a sort of couch, he found. He glanced around the interior of the poor hut, through the open door at the sparkling sea.

"What—" he began.

"I found you yesterday, *señor*, far out to sea, riding on a piece of wreckage," the native said. "You had lost your wits. You fought me when I tried to take you into my boat, and tried to draw blade against me. Then you went unconscious, and I had my way with you."

"And—and then?" Señor Zorro gasped.

"Why, *señor*, I fetched you here!" the native explained. "And throughout the night you raved, and so far to-day. The sun has but two more hours to live."

"More water!" Zorro commanded.

The native gave it him. He drank deeply, stood up, walked to the door and looked out. There was no other habitation as far as he could see.

"Where is this?" Zorro asked.

"On the coast, *señor*, far to the south of Reina de Los Angeles. I am but a poor neophyte who eats what fish he can catch. Once I worked on a *hacienda, señor*, but the governor took all for taxes."

"I know," Señor Zorro told him.

"And so I got me a boat and came down the coast and built this poor house. And here I live alone and am happy. There are times when I carry fish to the stronghold of the pirates, and trade them for some other things—"

"Ha!" Zorro cried. "The stronghold of the pirates? Where is that?"

"Less than ten miles down the coast, *señor*, in a little bay. There are huts, and women and children, and every now and then the pirate ship puts in after a raid. They are safe there, *señor*, though they are within eight miles of the *presidio* of San Diego de Alcála."

"By the saints!" Zorro swore. "And how does it come that you did not rob me of my sword and the few things of value upon me, and toss me into the sea?"

The native looked at him frankly. "Pardon, *señor*," he said, "but I never would do such a thing as that. For I knew you instantly, *señor*. You are Señor

Zorro, who rode up and down El Camino Real and avenged the wrongs of the natives and *frailes*. You once punished a soldier who beat my father. If it is necessary, *señor*, I am ready to die that you may live."

"And now—"

"Now," the native interrupted, "it would be best for the *señor* to sit and rest, while I prepare some hot food. Then whatever he commands shall be done."

"There was a pirate ship in the offing, and another," Zorro insinuated.

"*Sí, señor!* The pirate ship ran from the other, going out to sea. But a short time ago I saw her pass, going toward the bay where the pirates have their headquarters. And the other ship passed but a short time ago, pursuing."

"By the saints!" Zorro cried. "I would go to this pirates' den of which you speak, and as speedily as possible."

"The *señor* must eat first, so that he will have strength," the native said, firmly. "Then I will guide the *señor* to the spot. It is ten miles, and the *señor* is a weak man."

"I will eat the food gladly," Zorro replied. "Do you prepare it as speedily as possible. There shall be an ample reward."

"It is reward enough that I have been able to save the *señor's* life," the native answered. "The friends of Señor Zorro do not forget what he did for them!"

SIXTEEN
SINGING CABALLEROS

BARBADOS WAS like a maniac after the pirate craft swung away from the trading schooner. He shrieked at his men to make sail, and they needed but little urging. The fear of the supernatural was upon them, superstition ruled their minds.

Gradually they crept away from the schooner, but Barbados continued to watch her closely. He saw the new sails going aloft, and realized that there would be a pursuit. So he turned out to sea and began running for it.

He did not attempt to explain things to himself. He knew that his men outnumbered those on the schooner, and he felt reasonably sure that, in an engagement, the pirate crew would emerge victorious. Yet something seemed to tell him that the proper thing was to avoid the engagement if possible.

"We will lose that sorry craft in the wide waters," he told Sanchez, "and then we will turn and go to the rendezvous. There we'll unload and apportion the loot, and care for the wench until the man comes to claim her. If we are followed, we can outfight the *caballeros* on land. The ghost of a man drowned in the sea is powerless on land, I have heard."

"And, if they follow us ashore—" Sanchez questioned.

"Then we fight them, fool," Barbados said. "You are still shaking like a child! A pirate—you? Ha! By my naked blade, you are no better than a woman in this business!"

"Men are men, but it is not in my mind to fight with ghosts," Sanchez told him. "We are bedeviled for some reason!"

"Ha!" Barbados gasped. "That reminds me!" He turned away and walked the length of the deck, and finally came across the man he sought, and drew him aside. "You have the thing yet?" he asked.

"The goblet? *Sí, señor!* If the captain wishes it—"

"Do not even show it to me!" Barbados commanded. "I would have you toss it into the sea, save that such an act might bring worse luck yet. So long as you retain it, perhaps you draw all the ill fortune to yourself. Spawn of hell, if ever you come face to face with that old *fray*, in flesh or in spirit, have a look to yourself! For you have done an evil thing!"

Barbados passed on, and descended to the cabin where Señorita Lolita had been returned a prisoner.

She was as a woman stunned. She had fainted when Señor Zorro had plunged into the sea, and Sanchez had carried her below. And when she regained consciousness she remained on the bunk and groaned and prayed by turns.

And now, when Barbados opened the door, she sat up quickly, a look of agony in her face. One thing she had done—picked up from the floor of the cabin the dagger that had belonged to the man Señor Zorro had slain through the crack. She had cleaned it, and thrust it in the bosom of her dress, where it was out of sight, but where she could reach it instantly.

Barbados looked at her for a moment, and then spoke.

"In your right mind again, eh wench?" he said. "We are running away from your friends, and there can be no hope of rescue. It would be proper for you to make the best of it. The man for whom we have stolen you perchance will be kind."

"Foul beast and murderer!" the *señorita* said.

"Ha!" Barbados gasped. "I have been called worse things than that—things that you do not know exists, wench! Think you to hurt my tough hide with words?"

"Have you no manhood?" she asked. "Is it an honor for a score of men to take a girl captive? You struck down my father and burned my home! You sent to his death the man I love—"

"There are other men," said Barbados, "and other homes. And I did not strike down your father—Sanchez did that. From what he tells me, the blow was not a fatal one."

"You are the chief of murderers and thieves, the one responsible," she said.

"Words do not hurt my tough hide, I have said. It were best for you to be calm."

"Calm?" The *señorita* crept from the bunk, weak and staggering, her face white, her lips trembling, a suspicion of tears in her eyes. "Calm?" she repeated. "And how can you expect me to be calm? What is there in the future for me, save dishonor or death? When the moment comes, it will not take me long to choose!"

"Ha! When the moment comes, you may change your mind!"

"He whom you sent to death in the sea was worth ten score of you!" she cried, stepping closer to him. "And each of his friends who follow in that other ship are worth ten score of you! Do you think that you can escape them forever?"

"I can have them wiped from the face of the earth!" Barbados replied.

"Escape them, possibly—but not me!" she cried. "I have seen you kill the thing I love! And so—"

She clutched at her breast and drew forth the dagger. She gave a cry of rage, and struck out wildly. Barbados, caught unaware, lurched quickly to one side, but the blade struck his arm and tore away flesh and skin and brought a gush of blood.

"By my naked blade—" he swore.

He whirled as she struck again and missed, grasped her, and tore the dagger from her hand. He tossed her back upon the bunk, where she braced herself against the wall, gasping, weeping, expecting that now he would make an end of her.

But the pirate chief merely slipped the dagger into his belt, glanced at his wounded arm, swore again, and then stepped back to the door.

"A wench with spirit, eh?" he said. "Ha! I would not be this Captain Ramón and have the taming of you! Glad will I be when I turn you over to him! I have battles enough on my hands without fighting women! I'll send a man soon with food. Such a female warrior must eat to conserve her strength!"

He laughed at her, mocked her, went out and closed the door, and she heard the heavy bar shot into place and the sounds of his feet retreating. She collapsed on the bunk and gave way to a tempest of tears.

"Diego!" she breathed. "Diego, beloved!"

Barbados ascended to the deck, bathed the wound in his arm, and said nothing when Sanchez questioned him. Throughout the day he gave his attention to the sailing of the ship, but he could not shake off the schooner which followed.

Then came the night, and once more Barbados cursed the bright moon. For, though his craft showed no lights, yet could she be seen from the schooner. Back and forth Barbados sailed, but always failing to shake off the other ship. And when there came the dark hour before dawn he changed his course abruptly, and ran before the breeze.

But when the dawn came there was the schooner, a greater distance away, but still in sight. And so Barbados put off to sea again, for he wished, if it were possible, to go to the land rendezvous without drawing his foes there. Else he slew all of them, news of the pirates' headquarters would leak out, and they would have to move.

He ran before the wind, he tacked, he beat in toward the shore, out to sea, to the north and the south and the west. Now he gained, and now the schooner gained upon him. He cursed and drove his men, but they could accomplish nothing.

And finally he started running down the coast, intent upon reaching the rendezvous. If the men of the schooner dared follow him to land, they would be annihilated, he promised. Once or twice he felt like turning and forming an attack, but thoughts of the ghost of Señor Zorro deterred him.

"A sea ghost cannot fight on land!" Barbados told himself. "On land I have them at my mercy!"

The day started to die, and the pirate craft rushed down the coast with the schooner in close pursuit. It was almost nightfall when Barbados and his men guided the ship into the little bay. The schooner was some miles behind.

The anchor dropped, the ship swung broadside to the shore. From the land came sounds of a tumult, and down into the surf rushed men and women and children. The pirates' stronghold could be seen back some distance from the water.

There was a wide expanse of beach, a deep open space fringed with stubby trees and brush. Hills landlocked the scene. A score of huts dotted the edge of the flat. Fires were burning on the shore, stock ran wild among the habitations.

Overside went the boats, and the pirates commenced handing down the loot. Shrieks and calls came from the women and children on the shore, from the men who had been left behind as guards.

Barbados went ashore in the first boat, and began issuing his commands. The camp was to be put in a state for defense, he explained. Guards were to be established on the three land sides, and other men would watch the sea. The ship was warped closer to the shore, so that she could be defended easily.

Just as the night descended, the trading schooner sailed across the mouth of the bay, and presently she returned, farther out to sea. Barbados boarded the ship again, and took the *señorita* from her cabin. Sanchez lashed her wrists behind her.

"You go ashore, wench!" Barbados said. "And there you are to be held until such a time as this Captain Ramón comes to claim you. Why he should want you is more than I can explain to myself. You are a pretty wench, it is true, but too much of a spitfire!"

He watched her closely when she was in the boat. And when they landed the pirates' women and the ragged children rushed forward to jeer at her as she passed beside the flaming fire. Barbados took her to a large adobe building, the best structure in the camp. He opened the door and thrust her inside.

A woman cooking over an open fire whirled to look at him. She looked at the *señorita*, too, and her eyes flamed.

"What is this?" she demanded, her fists against her hips. "Is it a younger and prettier woman?"

"It is, indeed, Inez," Barbados laughed. "She is a share of the loot!"

"Your share, eh? And you dare to fetch her here?"

"Why not?" Barbados asked.

"To my face?" the woman screeched. She was of middle age, a creature hideous in a way. "So! It has come at last, has it? I am to be tossed aside for a comely wench you have stolen from some rich *hacienda*!"

"Jealousy is a foolish thing," Barbados observed. "Think you, Inez, to hold my love for life?"

"None other shall have it!" the woman screeched. She flashed forward, her hand raised to strike, her nails ready to tear into the *señorita's* fair face. But Barbados seized her and tossed her roughly aside.

"Peace!" he cried. "I want none of the wench! She is to be kept a prisoner until claimed. A share of the loot she is, but not my share. She was stolen for a great man!"

"This is the truth?" the woman asked.

"Do I generally speak falsehood?" Barbados thundered. "Enough! Put her in the storeroom, and feed her well. Treat her gently. She must be in prime condition when she is claimed. We were followed by a schooner upon which are *caballeros* striving to rescue her. She must not be rescued!"

The woman grinned horribly. She opened the door of a room adjoining and motioned for the *señorita* to enter. She stepped aside, and Lolita Pulido, looking straight ahead, her eyes fixed and glistening, went into the storeroom without speaking, her head held proudly.

Barbados hurried outside again. The black night had descended, but soon the moon was shining. Guards were sent into the fringe of woods, and a watchman to the summit of a hill in the rear. Men were posted on the ship, men walked around the huts, alert, ready to repel an attack.

But there came no attack during the night. The trading schooner had run down the coast and back, and then anchored two miles north of the bay.

"I know the place," the captain told Don Audre Ruiz. "Once some years ago I ran in there during a storm. Their camp must be in the open, and there will be no advantage in the attack. There can be no surprise, of course."

"What is your good advice?" Don Audre asked.

"That you land here with your *caballeros*, approach the camp and wait for the dawn. I'll land as many of my crew as can be spared from the ship, and let them circle the camp to attack from the other side. There must be men enough held here to get the schooner to sea for a run if the pirate craft comes out at us."

"That is agreed!" Don Audre said.

"But it will be a sorry business, Don Audre! You will be outnumbered three to one. And you may be sure that there are men in the camp who were not on the pirate ship. They may have a few pistols they have captured from ships, but it will be hand to hand work with blades. Three to one, at least, Don Audre!"

Don Audre Ruiz drew himself up. "Three beasts to one *caballero,*" he said. "It is an equal affair. There can be no hesitating, *señor*. Señorita Lolita Pulido is held a captive by those beasts. And I am not forgetting what happened to Don Diego, my friend! There is but one thing to do—attack! At least, we can die!"

There was a short conference, and then the boats began carrying the men to the shore. The *caballeros* approached to within a mile of the pirate camp and stopped to rest, sending scouts on ahead. The men of the crew circled to the other side.

Some of the *caballeros* slept, sprawled on the sand. But Don Audre Ruiz sat beside a tiny fire he had kindled, his knees drawn up and nursing them with his hands.

"At least we can die, Diego!" he said, softly. "And we can strive mightily before we do that!"

The black hour came, and then the first finger of the dawn. Don Audre arose and stretched himself, and walked for a time up and down the beach. The *caballeros* shook off their sleep, bathed their faces at the edge of the sea, exercised their muscles, whipped out their blades and fanned the air.

Sergeant Gonzales, who had snored throughout the night, snorted as he bathed his face and hands, and then strode down to Don Audre and confronted him.

"*Señor,* you are in command of this enterprise," the sergeant said. "There are orders?"

"Only that every man is to do his best," Don Audre replied. "The *señorita* is to be rescued if it is possible, and returned to the schooner."

"And the pirates are to be hanged?"

"Any that do not fall by our swords and are captured."

"Ha! It is a nuisance to hang a man!" Gonzales declared: "We would have to go to the ship for a rope. The blade is better! Fray Felipe!"

"*Señor?*" the fray questioned. He approached them.

"You are yet my friend," Gonzales said. "If you get into the thick of it, stand you behind me, that I may protect you. But a battle is not a place for a *fray*. Stay you behind, and say your prayers!"

"There is the matter of the goblet," Fray Felipe replied, softly.

"By the saints, I take it upon myself to get the goblet for you, *fray*!"

"Do so, and I call you son!"

Sergeant Gonzales bared his head for an instant. He looked at Fray Felipe as though embarrassed, and then returned his hat to his head and gulped. "I have been an evil man in my time," he said, "but I trust that the saints will forget it for this day at least. I would have added strength to this good right arm of mine! Don Audre, I am ready!"

Don Audre Ruiz led the way along the shore. They crept nearer the camp of the pirates, spread out fan fashion, and approached boldly. They reached the crest of a slope, and saw the camp spread before them in the first rays of the morning sun.

The pirates seemed to be more numerous than even Don Audre Ruiz had expected. It looked to be a hopeless task, this attack. But there was something to urge them on.

They stopped to look at one another. In silks and satins and plumes they were, with their jeweled swords at their sides. And before them the stronghold, with the ragged, dirty pirates there ready to give battle.

"If Señor Zorro were only here to lead us!" Don Audre Ruiz said, with a sigh. "But he is not—and let us remember why he is not—and strike the harder because of our remembrance! If you are ready—"

He whipped out his gleaming blade and waved it above his head, and the *caballeros* drew blades in turn, and answered him with their cheers.

And so they advanced to the attack—slowly, carefully, in a perfect line. And Don Audre Ruiz, because he wanted to give himself and the others added courage, and because he felt that it was fitting, sang lustily a song of old:

"Singing *caballeros*, going forth to die!
Laughing in the face of grinning Death!
Facing task that's hopeless, ready yet to try!
Singing with the last of earthly breath!"

The *caballeros* took up the refrain and sang it through to the end, their voices ringing across the sea and the land. And, the song at an end, they were grim and silent again, intent upon the bloody business before them. The pirates were preparing, they could see. In a very few minutes the clash would come.

And suddenly, from the distance, from the slope between the two attacking forces, came a solitary voice, also raised in song:

"*Atención!* A *caballero's* near—"

They glanced up, astounded. Running down the slope toward them came a figure they knew well. Don Audre Ruiz gave a great cry of joy and thankfulness. The *caballeros* cheered, and wept unashamed. For well they knew the singer and the song.

"Zorro!" they cried. "Zorro!"

And so they rushed to the attack!

PART FOUR

PART IV

SEVENTEEN
A WILD RIDE

THE PIRATES evidently had decided to make the fight at some little distance from their huts and adobe houses, so they rushed forward, shrieking their battle-cries, brandishing their weapons, shouting and cursing to give themselves courage. The great voice of Barbados rolled out above the din in a multitude of commands. The shrill voice of Sanchez echoed him.

The *caballeros* advanced in a perfect line, their shining blades held ready, grim and silent now, their minds intent upon the bloody business confronting them. Señor Zorro, they could see, was making his way down the slope toward them as speedily as possible, shouting that he was coming, still singing bits of his song between his shouts.

The pirates had a few firearms, but little ammunition for them. And they were more used to fighting hand-to-hand with naked blades. Yet they discharged their firearms first as the *caballeros* advanced, and took a bloody toll. The *caballeros* had nothing but their blades, for they had come from Don Diego Vega's bachelor supper, and they had worn no firearms to that affair.

There was a moment of silence pregnant with dire possibilities, the lull before the storm—and then the two forces met with a crash! Blades clanged together, men gasped and fought and fell.

The line of the *caballeros* was broken almost immediately, and each found himself the particular foe of three or more pirates. Yet they fought like maniacs, silently at times, right merrily at times, feeling that they were doomed, but determined to do what damage they could before the battle went entirely against them.

And then there was a sudden tumult on the opposite side of the pirates' camp, and into it and among the huts charged the crew of the trading schooner, the captain at their head.

But the pirates were so great in numbers that they were disconcerted only for an instant. From the huts and the adobe buildings poured men Barbados had been general enough to hold in reserve. The crew of the trading schooner was overwhelmed. The men of the sea fought valiantly, but they died with their captain.

And now Señor Zorro had reached the bottom of the slope, and, blade in hand, rushed to join his friends. His sword flashed as he entered the fight and tried to turn the tide of battle. His shouts rang out above the bedlam.

"Ha!" he cried. "At the scum, *caballeros*! They cannot stand against proper men!"

"Ha!" roared the great voice of Sergeant Gonzales, as he fought off two of the pirate crew with his long sword. "To me, Señor Zorro! We'll carve a pathway through the swine!"

But Señor Zorro did not hear him. He had seen that his old friend, Don Audre Ruiz, was sorely pressed, and he fought his way quickly to Don Audre's side. His blade seemed to be half a score as it flashed in and out and downed one of Don Audre's opponents. Like a man possessed, Señor Zorro pressed forward again, straight at the pirates in the foreground.

"*Atención!* A *caballero's* near—"

He sang it as he fought, stopping the song now and then for an instant to grunt as he made an unusually hard thrust. The men before him broke and fled, and Señor Zorro, with Don Audre at his side, seized the minor advantage of the moment. The other *caballeros* rallied and followed.

"The ghost!" one of the pirates shrieked. "It is the ghost from the sea!"

"Ha!" Señor Zorro cried, and cut down another man. "Ha, scum! So you fear ghosts? Have at you—"

"Pirates, eh?" Sergeant Gonzales was crying, puffing and blowing out his great cheeks as he fought. "Stand, pirates, and fight like men! Is this a fight or a test of speed, dolts and fools? Meal mush and goat's milk!"

"A ghost!" another man shrieked.

Barbados whirled around in time to see Sanchez, a look of terror in his face, about to retreat. He took in the situation at a glance.

"It is no ghost, fiends of hell!" he shrieked at his men. "'Tis this Señor Zorro somebody has saved from the sea! At him! Fetch him to me alive! Does a ghost fight with a blade that runs red? Get the fiend!"

His words carried weight. The pirates gathered their courage and surged forward again. The other men came running from the huts and the adobe buildings, now that the crew of the trading schooner had been handled. The *caballeros* found their line broken once more, found that they were being scattered.

Still side by side, Señor Zorro and Don Audre Ruiz fought as well as they could. But here in the open they could not get their backs against a wall. However, they did the next best thing—they stood back to back and engaged a circle of foes.

The fight swirled around them. Señor Zorro's face wore an expression of anxiety now. He knew, fully as well as did Don Audre Ruiz, that this wonderful show of courage and blade skill was availing the *caballeros* nothing. Slowly but surely, the pirates were traveling the road to triumph.

Señor Zorro was of gentle blood, and could have died as well as the best of them, a song upon his lips and laughter in his eyes. But he felt at this juncture that his life was not his own to throw away recklessly. Did he die with his friends, the *señorita* would have none to give her aid.

He would have to live, to win free if the tide of battle was against him, and then take his chance at being able to return and rescue his lady. He glanced around quickly as he fought. More than half the *caballeros* had been wounded or slain. And still more pirates were rushing forward, it appeared, with the intention of making an end of things.

And now there came an added menace. Among the huts there was a ramshackle corral, in which the pirates had put a number of blooded horses stolen from *hacienda* owners. And now some of the fighting men crashed against the insecure fencing and demolished it, and the animals, frightened at the din of battle, rushed through the broken place and into the open.

The fighting men, the clashing of blades, the shouts and screams seemed to infuriate the beasts. The smell of blood was in their nostrils. The horses charged wildly through the throng, upsetting *caballeros* and pirates alike. One noble stallion brushed aside the foes of Señor Zorro and Don Audre Ruiz, but separated them also. Their enemies rushed toward them again before they could get together—and they were no longer back to back.

Their case was desperate now. Each was surrounded and overwhelmed. Señor Zorro fought with what skill he could, keeping a wide circle with his flashing blade. He heard the voice of Sergeant Gonzales roaring in the distance. He heard, also, the thunderous voice of Barbados.

"Alive! Take them alive!" the pirate chief was screeching. "There will be rich ransom! Ransom and torture! Take them alive, fiends!"

Sanchez echoed the command, and the pirates shrieked in answer that they understood. And Señor Zorro and his friends understood also. The pirates would have rare sport baiting *caballeros* who were not ransomed speedily enough to suit them. Revenge and profit would be their lot.

The *caballeros* wasted no breath in speech. They had heard, and well they understood the meaning. They fought like maniacs, and maimed and slew their men. But there was no chance of ultimate victory, for the numbers against them were too great.

Here and there in the open space a chorus of fiendish shrieks told that a captive had been taken, his sword whipped from his hand. Señor Zorro suddenly found himself hard pressed, but fought free and made an effort to reach the side of Don Audre Ruiz again. But that was no easy feat, he discovered.

"Get that Señor Zorro!" Barbados was shouting. "A reward to the men who fetch him to me alive! Ha! This time we'll make a ghost of him indeed!"

Señor Zorro knew a touch of despair for a moment, but he fought it off quickly. If he were captured, the Señorita Lolita would have no protector, and would be at the mercy of these fiends and Captain Ramón. Were it not better to escape, to make an effort to return later, than to fight until death at the side of his friend?

"Audre!" he cried.

"*Sí?*"

"Can you win free?"

"The curs surround me!"

"One of us must win free!" Zorro cried. "There is the *señorita* to be considered!"

"Get away, Don Diego, my friend!" Audre Ruiz shouted. "Save yourself, and the saints bless you—"

"I will return!" Señor Zorro shouted the promise. "Let the beasts take you, Audre! Alive, you may be of some service! Dead—you are gone forever!"

Señor Zorro did not listen for an answer. Two determined pirates were before him. But they hesitated in their attack, because they were eager to take him alive and so gain the reward that Barbados had promised. And their hesitation gave Señor Zorro the opportunity he desired.

He hurled himself forward, stretched one man on the ground and put the other in momentary flight. Others rushed at him from the side, and for an instant, as he turned, he had a vision of Don Audre Ruiz being disarmed. And then he whirled again, darted swiftly away, fighting to clear a path.

Down toward him rushed the big stallion, still frightened because of the din of battle. Señor Zorro swept another man from before him and sprang at the horse. He went upon the animal's back, lurched sickeningly for an instant, and righted himself. His balance regained, he kicked at the flanks of his mount. It was all that he could do. The horse was without saddle or bridle, without even a halter.

The animal hesitated, and Señor Zorro kicked again with what strength he could. And the horse, suddenly terrified, sprang forward like some supernatural beast. The pirates went down before him and before Señor Zorro's blade.

Up the slope the big stallion started, almost running down Sergeant Gonzales and the pirates who had already taken him prisoner. Past Fray Felipe he sprang, and Señor Zorro saw the aged *fray's* hand raised in blessing.

Like a wild animal the stallion dashed at a group of the victorious pirates, who shrieked and scattered to either side. Señor Zorro rode erect, his sword flashing, and he was laughing wildly, like a man on the verge of hysterics.

"*Señores!* Have you ever seen this one?" he screeched.

He leaned to one side as the plunging horse went forward, locked his heels in the animal's flanks. He grasped one of the pirates and lifted him from the ground, whirled him around and sent him flying through space.

He would have guided the animal back and made an effort to disconcert his foes further, but the horse could not be guided. And so Señor Zorro rode on up the slope and away from the pirates' camp—rode his fiery, unmanageable mount straight at the fringe of trees on the top of the hill.

From the distance came Barbados, fiendish, cursing, because the man he most wanted to capture had made an escape.

And Señor Zorro answered it, also from a distance, with a burst of song:

"*Atención!* A *caballero's* near—"

EIGHTEEN
HOPE IS CRUSHED AGAIN

SEÑORITA LOLITA PULIDO passed into the store room of the adobe building with her head erect and a look of pride in her face, as has been said. But when the heavy door was closed behind her, and she heard a bar dropped into place, she changed swiftly.

For a moment she leaned against the door, listening to Barbados and Inez, his woman. Then Barbados went away, and the woman also, and the *señorita* dropped upon a stool that happened to be in one corner of the room, and buried her face in her hands.

There seemed no hope left. Señor Zorro, Don Diego Vega, her beloved, was at the bottom of the sea, she supposed. She was in the hands of these pirates, being kept a prize for a man she detested and loathed. There seemed no way of escape.

But the *señorita* had determined her course. She would die rather than be shamed, she told herself. She would join Don Diego in the land of to-morrow, be his celestial bride. The blood of the Pulidos coursed her veins, and told her to do that.

It was dark in the store room, but presently the door was opened and the woman Inez entered with a small torch made of palm fiber and tallow. She fastened the torch to the wall, went out again, and returned with food. A jug of water, some poorly cooked goat flesh and a pulpy mass, the like of which the *señorita* never had seen before, constituted the meal.

"Eat, wench!" Inez commanded. "Eat, and drink your fill of the water! A dainty morsel you are, but there be some men who like women of a different sort. Ha! 'Twould do you no good to make merry eyes at my Barbados!"

The *señorita* scarcely understood, for she had not been taught to make eyes at any man. She drank deeply of the water, for she was thirsty, and she wanted to eat, but did not like the appearance of the food.

"Too dainty for pirate fare, eh?" Inez sneered, rubbing her fat nose with a forefinger. "Wait until real hunger gnaws at your stomach, pretty wench, and then you'll eat!"

The *señorita* got up from the stool suddenly and stepped forward. Her hands were at her sides, her chin was raised, there was pleading in her face.

"You are a woman," she said, softly. "In your heart there must be some sympathy for other women."

"Not much," Inez acknowledged. "Few women have shown sympathy or kindness toward me. I was a poor girl working on a *hacienda*, and listened to the lies of a handsome traveler. And when my fault was discovered it was the women who turned their backs. A woman of your class, wench, kicked me out!"

"That is the way of the world," Lolita told her. "Still, you must have in your breast some inkling of pity. Would see the thing happen to me that is going to happen if I cannot avoid it?"

"Ha!" Inez laughed. "What would you?"

"Help me get away!" the *señorita* begged. "Help me to be free, and in some manner I'll get up El Camino Real to Reina de Los Angeles. I have friends. In time I'll send you more money than Barbados will get from Captain Ramón."

"And Barbados would take the money from me, slit my throat, and find him another woman," Inez replied, laughing coarsely. "I know nothing of his business deals with Captain Ramón or any other. Nor do I care to know them!"

"Have you no pity?"

"I have nothing to do with it," the woman declared. "I have orders to give you water and food and a light, and I have done so. That is the end."

Before the *señorita* could speak again the woman had gone out and closed the door. Señorita Lolita heard the bar dropped into place once more. She went slowly back to the stool, and managed to eat a few morsels of the goat's flesh, after which she drank more of the water.

By the light of the torch she inspected her prison room. There was nothing in it except some old casks that once had contained olives and tallow. There was but the one door, and only a single window, and the window was small and had bars of metal across it.

Escape was impossible, the *señorita* decided. She went back to the stool again, and sat upon it and buried her face in her hands once more. The future seemed to hold nothing but death and disgrace, and she knew how to choose between them, if the chance was given her.

Tired, exhausted by the events of the day, she found sleep descending upon her. She left the stool and curled up in a corner on the floor, determined to keep awake. But she could not. Her head nodded, and after a time she fell asleep.

A din awakened her. The torch had burned out and the light of day was pouring through the little window. The little *señorita* was stiff and uncomfortable. She got up and hurried to the window, and by standing upon one of the empty casks managed to peer out of it.

She could see a portion of the camp. The pirates were arming themselves and rushing here and there like madmen. She could hear the great voice of Barbados as he issued his commands. And then there was a lull, and she heard singing in the distance. Another lull and she heard a single voice raised in song:

"*Atención!* A *caballero's* near—"

Her heart almost stopped beating for a moment. But in the next instant she told herself that she had been foolish to hope. It was Señor Zorro's song, but he was dead at the bottom of the sea. And other *caballeros* knew it. It was some *caballero* singing in the distance. But that gave her a small measure of hope, for it meant that Don Diego's friends were at hand and would make an effort to rescue her.

There was another time of comparative silence, and then the battle began. The *señorita* could see none of it at first, for she was on the wrong side of the building. But she could hear the shrieks and cries, the ringing of blades, the screeches of pain and curses of anger.

She saw the crew of the schooner attack from the other side, and shrieked her horror as the pirates cut them down. And then the fight was out of her sight again.

Down from the cask she dropped. She ran across to the door and pounded upon it with her tiny fists, struck it repeatedly, until her hands were cut and bleeding. After a time it was opened, and the woman Inez stood before her, thrust her away and entered.

"What is it, wench?" she demanded. "More food and water?"

"No!" she gasped. "I—what is taking place? There is so much confusion—"

"A battle is taking place, wench!" the woman declared, bracing her fists against her hips. "Some *caballeros* came in a ship and saw fit to attack the camp. Many of them will see nothing more."

"And—and the battle—"

"How goes it, mean you? Ha, wench! The *caballeros* are being cut down, of course. We have them three to one! Some are to be taken prisoners, some held for ransom, others tortured. It will be a lesson to the men of gentle blood not to fight with pirates! Gentlemen are only gentlemen—but men are men!"

"Gentlemen are always gentlemen, and sometimes mere men are beasts," the *señorita* told her.

"How is this? Do you want me to rock your head with a blow, wench? Ha! There will be rare sport if this Señor Zorro is taken prisoner."

"Zorro?" the *señorita* gasped.

"The same, wench! You were to wed with him, I have been told. Ha! He'll not be ready for his wedding when Barbados has finished with him!"

"Señor Zorro is dead!"

"I know that he walked the plank. And the fools thought that he was a ghost when he appeared here. But somebody must have saved him from the sea. He's out there now, fighting. They will make a captive of him!"

The *señorita's* heart beat wildly. Then it had been Zorro she had heard singing in the distance!

But in the next instant she told herself that it could not be. Zorro had walked the plank with a weight fastened to his wrists. The pirates were mistaken. It was some other *caballero* who looked like Señor Zorro, who fought as he fought, and acted as he acted.

She threw aside the momentary hope, and crept toward the woman Inez again. If the fight was going against the *caballeros*, if the pirates were to be victors, she had scant time.

The *señorita* began acting as she never acted before, and though she was new to the game, her woman's intuition, her terror and her desperate need served her well.

"So the pirates are to win!" she said, laughing lightly. "And there will be a lot of ransom money and loot."

"How is this?" Inez shrieked. "You, a prisoner, seem joyful that the rescue is not accomplished."

"I am a prisoner—*sí*!" the *señorita* said. "But perhaps I shall be more soon."

"What mean you?" the woman gasped.

"Perhaps it might have been in my mind that it would be better to have a real man than wed a gentleman of noble blood. Is it not peculiar that Barbados took me the night before my wedding?"

"Ha! Can you speak with plain meaning?" the woman asked.

"Did you believe the story of Captain Ramón?" the *señorita* demanded. "I did, too, at first! And then I thought differently. You are getting old, you see, and fat."

"Wench!" the woman cried, threatening her.

"If you strike me, Barbados will punish!"

"Barbados punish me? Ha!"

"Are you so easily fooled?" the *señorita* asked. "It is plain to me what is to happen. Barbados means to have me for himself. There is no escape. So I may as well make the best of it. And since I am to be the woman of the pirate chief, I must be loyal to him. If things must be so, is it strange that I hope he gets much ransom and loot?"

"By the devils of Hades!" the woman swore. "If I thought this to be truth—"

"Can you not see that it is?" the *señorita* queried. "Captain Ramón may have dealings with Barbados, but it does not follow that Captain Ramón is to have me. That was just a little falsehood to fool you, possibly."

"Ha! So you would take my place?" the woman cried.

The *señorita* recoiled as the other approached, and held up one of her hands.

"I have no desire to take your place," she declared. "But since I cannot help myself, what else is there to do?"

"I could kill you with my bare hands!"

"And then Barbados would kill you in turn and go find himself another woman."

"Ha! I could kill him!"

"You could not!" the *señorita* said.

The woman Inez was quiet for a moment, and then: "You are right—I could not," she replied.

"There is a way."

"And how, wench?"

"Help me to escape," the *señorita* said. "If I am gone, you are in safe possession of the affections of Barbados. He will not raid again soon, will not soon have a chance to find him another woman. And you can, in the meantime, win back his love again."

"Ha! If I aid you to escape he will kill me!"

"Make it appear that I escaped myself," the *señorita* replied. "You are strong. You can tear out that window until it is large enough for me to get through. Let him think that there was some tool in the storeroom and that I did the work."

"Ha! If I thought you were speaking truth—"

"Very well!" said the *señorita*. "Wait and see whether it is the truth."

The woman hesitated, searching the *señorita's* face with her keen glance. Then she grunted and hurried into the other room, while Lolita Pulido waited in fear and trembling, wondering what was to come now. Had the woman gone to tell Barbados the story?

But presently Inez returned, and she carried a peculiar strip of iron with one sharp end, a bit of wreckage, perhaps, from some ill-fated ship.

"Watch you at the door, on the inside!" she commanded. "Do not go into the other room. They are still fighting and perhaps there will be time."

The *señorita* hurried across to the door, hope singing in her heart again. There she watched and listened to the din of battle. All would be well if she could escape in the confusion and get away from the camp. She could reach El Camino Real and make her way along it. If she could reach San Diego de Alcála, she would find friends.

She turned and looked at the woman. Inez was tearing out the masonry and adobe around the window. The metal bars already were inside the room and out of the way.

"Be quick!" the *señorita* said. "I am small, and do not need a very large space."

"It is done!" the woman replied.

She hurried back to the middle of the room, and the *señorita* turned to look. The aperture was large enough, she knew at a glance. She could crawl through, jump to the ground, go up the slope, and reach the fringe of trees that she could see in the distance. Once more hope came to her.

"I must have some old clothes—ragged and dirty clothes," she said. "I will leave some of these."

The woman did not reply, but she hurried from the storeroom with a gleam of avarice in her eyes. She was more than willing to trade ragged garments for some of silk and satin.

Back she came, after a time, and the *señorita* pulled off her gown and put on the ragged one, shuddering as she did so, not because of the rags but because of the dirt. She streaked her face with dirt from the floor, and washed her hands in it, disarranged her hair, and threw a ragged shawl over her head.

"A woman does not wear a torn shawl, a ragged dress, and fine slippers at the same time," Inez observed.

The *señorita* kicked off her slippers and thrust her feet into the filthy sandals the hag furnished her. She hurried to the window, the woman before her. But Inez grasped her by an arm and held her back.

"Not that way!" the woman gasped. "It is too late! That way is guarded!"

The heart of the *señorita* sank again. She scrambled to the top of the cask she had used before, and peered out. Within sight there were half a dozen men guarding that side of the camp against a possible surprise. If she got through the window they would see her, block her path up the slope and toward the trees, and investigate.

"Is there no way out?" the *señorita* cried in despair.

"There is only the front."

"Then let me out the front way. The men are fighting, and perhaps they will not notice me if I go out that way, and make haste up the slope."

"All women and children have been ordered to remain in the huts while there is fighting."

"They will do no more than shriek at me to get inside again," the *señorita* said. "I can pretend to be frightened, and run. I can get away, if you'll let me out!"

"And I be blamed for it!"

"Not so!" she cried. "Bar this door. I'll slip out the front, and they will think that I came around the building. You can pretend that you believe me to be in the store room. When they open the door and find me gone, find the window torn out, they'll think that I did it, and got out that way. If anybody is punished, it will be the guards outside."

"I am afraid!" the woman said.

"And are you not afraid, also, of seeing another woman in your place here?"

The face of Inez grew purple for an instant, and her eyes blazed. Suddenly she strode across to the door, opened it, and looked out upon the fighting. She closed the door again, and turned back to face the *señorita*.

"The fighting now is at some distance," she said. "There is a chance. Wait!"

She whirled around to bar the door of the storeroom. The little *señorita* waited, trying to be calm, though her heart was pounding at her ribs. She was to escape at last! She could get up the slope, hurry through the trees—

"You must use speed!" the woman was informing her. "And if you are caught, you must take all the blame. Barbados would kill me if he knew."

"Give me a dagger," the *señorita* begged. "Then, if I am caught, I'll do that which will render me speechless!"

"Ha!"

"I mean it! Death would be welcome to the other!"

The woman hesitated a moment, and then reached beneath her ragged shawl and drew a dagger out. The *señorita* clutched it, and hid it away in her bosom.

For another moment they faced each other. And then the woman Inez lurched across the room toward the door, the *señorita* trotting along at her heels.

And hope turned to black despair once more in the twinkling of an eye! For the door suddenly was thrown open, and before them stood—Captain Ramón!

NINETEEN
DOUBLE-FACED

THERE WAS a moment of astonishment for all three of them. Then the Señorita Lolita gave a little cry of mingled fright and despair, and recoiled against the wall. Señor Zorro dead, the pirates winning the battle against the *caballeros*, and before her the man she loathed and feared! The future seemed very dark, indeed.

"*Dios!*" she breathed.

But the woman Inez, after blinking her eyes at the unexpected apparition, screeched her rage and darted to a corner, where she picked up a heavy bar of iron. She whirled toward the intruder, the bar raised to strike. But Captain Ramón laughed and held up his hand.

"Do not be afraid of me, hag!" he told the woman. "I wear the uniform of the Governor's soldiery, it is true, but I am the good friend of Barbados! I am Captain Ramón, of Reina de Los Angeles!"

"Ha!" the woman gasped. She dropped the bar of iron and stood with arms akimbo. "So you are Captain Ramón?"

"*Sí!*"

"That must be true, else you would not have lived to get to this building," Inez said. "And why are you here?"

"To see the little lady standing behind you," Ramón said, smiling. "She has been kept safe, I see."

"You are to claim her?"

"What else?"

"Ha!" Inez gasped. It flashed through her mind, now, that Barbados really had no personal interest in the *señorita,* and she believed, also, that she had almost been tricked into aiding an important prisoner to escape. A glance at the *señorita's* face confirmed her suspicion, for Lolita was not acting now. Inez realized that she would have to speak quickly to save herself.

"You come in good time," she declared to the captain. "The wench has been kept in the storeroom. But an instant ago, hearing no sounds within, I unbarred and opened the door. And she had enlarged the window, and dressed in those rags. She intended escaping, *señor*! Had it not been for me now she would be gone."

"You have done well," Ramón declared. "That is the door to the storeroom?"

"*Sí!*" Inez answered. She dropped the bar and threw the door open. Captain Ramón peered inside, then turned and smiled again, first at the hag, and then at the *señorita.*

"It is indeed well," he said. "*Señorita,* you might have been injured on the outside, for men are fighting. And your present garments are scarce suited to your station in life. Your dainty face is streaked with dirt, too, and your hands soiled."

"Your presence soils me more!" the *señorita* said.

"You prefer pirates, *señorita*?"

"There are several grades of depravity," she said, "and pirates may not be the lowest."

"Ha! A biting tongue in a sweet face!" Captain Ramón declared.

"More biting than the blade you wear at your side, *señor*! Why do you not show your true colors? Why not go out and fight with your friends, the pirates and thieves and murderers, against men of gentle blood?"

Captain Ramón bowed in mockery. "If you will be kind enough to glance through the open door, *señorita,* you will perceive that the fighting is at an end," he replied. "What *caballeros* are not dead have been taken prisoners. And the women and children are mocking them. Go, hag, and mock with the others! I'll guard the *señorita* well."

He leered at the woman as he spoke, and she grinned and shuffled from the building. She was eager to get at Barbados and tell him how the *señorita* had attempted an escape, and how she, the loyal and faithful Inez, had prevented it.

"Into the storeroom, *señorita*!" Captain Ramón commanded when they were alone.

"I prefer this, *señor.*"

"Quickly!" he commanded. "We'll close the door. We do not wish to be overheard!"

"What mean you?"

"Can you not understand?" the captain cried. He thrust her before him into the storeroom, and closed the door behind him. He darted across to the window and looked out, acting mysteriously.

"If you would rid me of your foul presence—" the *señorita* began.

Captain Ramón whirled toward her. On the long, hot ride from Reina de Los Angeles, which had taken him the better part of two days, and during which he had not spared mounts, he had thought out everything.

He was playing a sort of double game, this Captain Ramón. He wished to reinstate himself in the good graces of better men, he wanted to make the *señorita* believe that he had rendered her a great service and try to win her regard openly, and he wished to aid his master, the Governor, in acquiring credit in the southland, where he had small credit now.

He had heard, on his way to the pirate camp, that Señor Zorro had walked the plank. He could take the helpless *señorita* now for his own, but if he did that he would have to become a renegade forever, live like an outcast. And Captain Ramón loved his uniform, and wealth and power.

So why not play the pirates and honest men against each other and make a double winning? He had had ample time to think it out. And so, as he faced the *señorita's* scorn, he pretended surprise that she did not understand.

"Foul presence, *señorita*?" he said. "After I have risked so much to be of service to you?"

"Of service to me?" she cried. "When I was abducted by your orders, when my home was burned and my father cut down?"

"Have the beasts told you that?" Ramón asked. "That is because Barbados knew I was infatuated with you. He believed I would thank him for doing such a thing."

"You are allied with pirates!" she accused.

"Listen, *señorita,* for the love of the saints!"

"The saints are better off your lips, *señor*!"

"Attend me!" he commanded again. "It is a game we have been playing."

"A sorry game!"

"*Señorita,* by your gentle blood I ask you to give me your ear! I have but pretended friendship with these pirates, that the soldiers may take them later, and hang them all."

"What monstrous falsehood is this?" she asked.

"I beg your attention, *señorita*! Some of them may be coming soon. I have pretended to be in league with them. They raided Reina de Los Angeles while I and my soldiers were gone. I have followed swiftly to rescue you. They think that I am a friend. But now, assured of your safety, I can act speedily. Let them continue thinking, for the time being, that I accept you as a prize. I shall ride away to San Diego de Alcála, which is but a few miles, fetch the troopers from there, rescue you, release the *caballeros* now held as prisoners, and wipe out this pirate brood!"

"But why—" she began.

"It was the only way, *señorita*. The soldiers are few, and the pirates have been able to strike the coast where there were no troopers handy. It is a trap that we have arranged for them. Perhaps it may not seem a gentle thing to do —but one cannot be gentle with pirates."

"I wish that I could believe you," she said.

"Believe me, *señorita*! I love you so much—"

"I am betrothed," she said simply.

"But I have grave news for you. I have been told that Don Diego Vega is no more, that these beasts forced him, as Señor Zorro, to walk the plank."

"I was there," she said, her eyes filling with tears. "I saw it. Nevertheless, I am betrothed to him, *señor*, now and forever, in life and in death!"

"That is because your grief is new," the captain said. "You are young, *señorita*, you have a life to live. If you would live it with me—"

"*Señor!*" she warned.

"I can understand why you dislike me a bit," he said. "Perhaps, in the past, I did some things that a gentleman should not do. But it was because of my great love for you, because I was afraid of losing you."

"*Señor*, let us talk of other things, if we must talk," the *señorita* begged.

"Do you not realize, *señorita*, that, if I wish it, you are in my power?"

"Now you are showing your true colors!" she said.

"Not so! I am showing you that I am not taking advantage of the situation," he declared. "I intend rescuing you and the friends these pirates now hold as prisoners. I am risking my life to do it. And, if I succeed, cannot you look upon me with some favor?"

"If I have misjudged you, *señor*, I am indeed sorry," she replied. "But it is useless to talk of such things. My heart is with Don Diego Vega, in life and in death!"

"Perhaps in the future—"

"There can be no hope, *señor*!"

Captain Ramón's face flushed and his eyes blazed for an instant. But he still had his game to play, the many-sided game that he hoped would result in great fortune.

"If you could only believe me!" he said.

"Perhaps—after you have demonstrated your loyalty."

"Then I go now to talk to Barbados, then to San Diego de Alcála for the troopers. Guard yourself well until my return. I must pretend that I wish you watched, kept from escaping. A false move, *señorita,* and all of us are lost!"

"I can only do as you say," she said. "I will be guarded in any case."

"Come into the other room. I'll call the hag! And I'll return to you before I ride for San Diego de Alcála, if there are more plans you should know."

Captain Ramón opened the door, bowed low as she passed through it, and looked after her with the corners of his lips curled. Then he hurried toward the front, calling for Inez.

TWENTY
THE UNEXPECTED

CAPTAIN RAMÓN BADE the woman guard the *señorita* well, and then hurried from the adobe building. Just in front of it he stopped to look over the scene. Dead men were scattered on the ground at a distance. There were more dead men around the huts, where the crew of the trading schooner had made their last stand.

The wounded were shrieking and groaning, and some of the pirates were giving them a rough surgery. Others were hurrying the *caballero* prisoners toward another adobe building, where they were to be kept. Women and children ran beside them, shrieking insults, hurling small stones. But the *caballeros* held their heads proudly, and laughed and jested with one another.

Captain Ramón darted to the end of the building, so he would not be seen by the prisoners. It was not in his mind to be suspected at the outset. The game he was playing was one of hazard, and he knew that the slightest mistake would be disastrous.

He had planned with Barbados to conduct the raid, and thereby had gained the pirate chief's confidence. And now he had further plans. He would tell Barbados that he would draw to the camp the troopers at San Diego de Alcála. Barbados and his men could ambush them and wipe them out. Then the pirates could cross the hills and raid and loot rich San Diego de Alcála.

But the captain intended no such thing in reality. Knowing how Barbados would prepare the ambush, he would lead the troopers in such a manner that the pirates would be wiped out to a man. Then the *caballeros* and the *señorita* could be rescued, and Captain Ramón would pose as their heroic rescuer. He hoped in this manner to regain the good will of the *caballeros* and a better standing with them, and to earn the gratitude of the *señorita* also.

Word of the exploit would run up and down El Camino Real. Men whose hands were now raised against the licentious and unscrupulous Governor would think better of him because the pirates had been wiped out. The Governor, in turn, would be grateful to Captain Ramón. And he would order Don Carlos Pulido, who was not dead of his wound, to give the hand of his daughter, Lolita, to Captain Ramón. Don Carlos scarce could refuse without endangering his fortunes further.

It was a pretty plot, the plot of a master rogue willing to sell friends and foes alike to advance his own interests. Captain Ramón grinned as he thought of it, and twirled his mustache, and marched around the corner of the building and across the open space toward where Barbados was standing and shouting orders concerning the disposition of the corpses.

And suddenly the captain found himself confronted by a man, and looked up quickly to see the burning eyes of old Fray Felipe fastened upon his face.

"What does an officer of the Governor in such a place, unless he be a prisoner of war?" Fray Felipe demanded.

Captain Ramón bowed before him. "Perhaps there are things that you do not understand, *fray*," he replied.

"And perhaps, *commandante*, there are things that I do understand!" Fray Felipe said. "Perhaps years of service in behalf of humanity have taught me to read a man's face and mind. Rogue, brute, traitor!"

"You are a *fray*, and wear a gown that should be respected, but do not tempt me too far!" Captain Ramón said angrily. "Say your prayers, and leave men's work to men!"

The captain bowed again, walked around the *fray*, and hurried to the side of Barbados.

"Ha!" the pirate cried. "You must have made haste to get here in such season."

"I almost killed two horses," the captain said.

"In such eager haste to see the wench, eh? And have you seen her?"

"She is safe and sound. She made an attempt to escape, but your woman stopped her."

"I wish you joy of the wench. There is too much of the fire of anger in her makeup to suit me," Barbados declared, laughing raucously. "She ripped my forearm with a dagger and killed one of my men aboard ship. The taming of her will take more than an hour's time, *commandante*!"

"Leave that to me!" Ramón said. "There are other things to be discussed now."

"And what?"

"Step aside!" Ramón commanded.

They walked some distance, to a spot where they would not be overheard.

"You know, certainly, the meaning of all this," Ramón said. "The Governor, who hates this southland, is eager to have it troubled as much as possible, even if he is forced to sacrifice a few of his own men."

"*Sí!*" Barbados said, both in question and in affirmation.

"See that the *señorita* is guarded well, and, in the meantime, before I think of such things as love, let us attend to more serious business."

"Is there a chance of profit?"

"How would you like to raid rich San Diego de Alcála when there would be small danger?"

The eyes of Barbados glistened. He knew a great deal about San Diego de Alcála. The town was rich, and the mission also. Wealth had been stored there since the earliest days of the missions.

"Attend me!" Ramón commanded. "You have here certain *caballeros* held as prisoners, and the *señorita* also. I'll go to San Diego de Alcála and spread the news at the presidio. I outrank the *commandante* there, and my words will be commands."

"I understand, *capitan*!"

"There are only a few troopers there now, the remainder having been sent to San Juan Capistrano to put down mutinous natives. I'll lead these troopers back to the pirate camp. Do you arrange an ambush at the head of the little cañon. I'll lead the men into it. You and your crew can cut them down. And then the way to San Diego de Alcála will be open to you!"

"By my naked blade—" Barbados swore.

"You must understand this thing, of course—it must look like a mistake. No man ever must think that the Governor had a hand in it, or that I did myself."

"I understand, *capitan*!"

"Then it is agreed?"

"*Sí!*"

"I'll have speech with the *señorita* again, and then ride like the wind. As soon as I have departed, arrange your men in the ambush. I'll return with the troopers before nightfall. You can wipe them out, attack San Diego de Alcála to-night, return, abandon this camp, and sail away and establish another on the coast of Baja California. You'll have wealth, women; your name will be spoken with respect!"

"*Sí!*" Barbados breathed. "It shall be as you say, *capitan*! And what share of the loot do you require?"

"Nothing whatever, if you keep the *señorita* safe for me."

"She shall be kept safe, I promise you!"

Captain Ramón whirled around and hurried back toward the adobe building. Inez had the *señorita* in the front room, guarding her well. She had just finished a tirade concerning the attempt of the *señorita* to engineer an escape through cunning words and implications.

Captain Ramón ordered the woman outside, and urged the *señorita* to go into the storeroom again.

"It is arranged," he said. "I ride for San Diego immediately. Do you continue to remain a prisoner, *señorita*, and save yourself from harm. Before the fall of night I'll be back with the troopers, this pirate brood will be wiped out, and you and the *caballeros* will be liberated. Then you can go up El Camino Real to your father."

"If you accomplish this thing, you shall have my gratitude," the *señorita* said.

"Nothing more than gratitude?"

"I have spoken concerning that, *señor*. There can be nothing but gratitude."

Captain Ramón suddenly whirled toward her. "It is something more than gratitude that I want!" he said. "Is your heart made of ice? Mine is flaming!"

"*Señor!*"

"What whim is it that makes you cling to the memory of a dead man?" he asked. "You are young, with a life before you."

"Please leave me with my sorrow, *señor*!"

"Then I may expect better treatment when your sorrow is somewhat dulled by time?"

"I am afraid not, *señor*."

"I risk my life in the service of you and your friends, and am to have no reward?"

"A man of gentle blood would not think of being rewarded for such a thing," she replied.

The face of Captain Ramón flushed and he took another step toward her. "I am sick of hearing so much of gentle blood," he said. "Mine is gentle enough, but it also can be hot at times. Am I a man to brook such nonsense? You owe me gratitude, and something more! One embrace, at least, here and now!"

"*Señor!*" she cried.

"Would you be so coy if the cursed Señor Zorro were here to beg a kiss?"

"More insults, *señor*?" she asked, her face flaming.

"Is it an insult for the daughter of an impoverished *don* to be kissed by one of his excellency's officers?"

"And would my father be impoverished were not his excellency a man of little honor?" she cried. "Poverty does not change the blood, *señor*!"

"More about your gentle blood, eh? And an affront to the Governor in your words, also? That calls for punishment, *señorita*! One embrace and then I ride!"

"I would rather die than have you touch me!" she cried. "You show your true colors again, *commandante*!"

"One embrace, and I make you forget this Señor Zorro!"

"If he were here, *señor*, you would not dare speak so!" she said. "You would cringe in terror, you who wear the mark of Zorro on your brow! It was for an insult to me that he put it there! It is like a coward to attack a helpless girl! If Señor Zorro were here—"

"But he is not here!" Ramón cried, laughing and leering at her. "And so—"

Again he started toward her, and her hand darted to her bosom to snatch out the dagger the woman Inez had given her earlier. But she did not draw out the dagger.

The window behind them suddenly was darkened, and the light shut off. Into the storeroom plunged a man who struggled to get free from the woman's clothes he wore over his own. As Captain Ramón recoiled and the *señorita* gave a little cry of fright the intruder's head flew up.

A blade flashed, the *señorita* found herself hurled to one side gently, and Captain Ramón found two eyes blazing into his—the eyes of Señor Zorro!

"Have you ever seen this one?" Señor Zorro demanded.

And, with his left hand, he slapped the *commandante* of the *presidio* of Reina de Los Angeles so that his head rocked!

TWENTY-ONE
FACE TO FACE

SEÑOR ZORRO, on the back of the infuriated and unmanageable stallion, had made his escape easily from the pirate camp. There was no question of him being overtaken, but for a time there was a grave question of Señor Zorro stopping the steed he rode.

Over the crest of the slope the animal beneath him plunged down into a ravine and galloped along it. Señor Zorro sheathed his sword and held on to the horse's mane. He bent low to avoid tree branches that promised to sweep him from the animal's back.

"*Dios!*" he muttered. "This is as bad as the battle!"

Some distance the frightened horse traveled, and then he made a great circle and returned toward the pirate camp. But Señor Zorro had no wish to return there too soon, lest he be captured in the vicinity. And so he waited until the horse, negotiating a slippery incline, slackened pace somewhat, and slipped easily from the animal's back.

The horse plunged on. Señor Zorro picked himself up, observed his scratches, and made a futile effort to brush his clothing. Then he walked to the crest of the slope and looked down toward the sea.

He was quite a way from the camp, but he could see it in the distance, see the dead and wounded on the ground, and a crowd of the pirates, with their women and children, in front of the adobe building that was being used as a prison.

Señor Zorro sat down to rest and watch. He knew that he was confronted by a dire emergency and a tremendous task, but he refused to admit it to himself. The *señorita* was down there, and she was to be rescued. And Don Audre Ruiz and the *caballeros* were there, to be rescued also.

Señor Zorro, after a breathing spell, got up and walked slowly along the crest of the slope among the stunted and wind-twisted trees, making certain that he could not be observed from the camp. He came a distance nearer, and watched for a time again. And he saw Captain Ramón!

If it had been in the mind of Señor Zorro to await the night before descending into the camp again that idea left his mind now. He hurried forward as speedily as possible, stopping now and then to listen, for fear some of the pirates may have been sent to search for him.

He did not know, could not think, how he was to enter the camp in the broad light of day without escaping discovery. And he could do little single-handed against the victorious pirate crew. Yet the plight of the little *señorita* called to him for action, and he knew that something should be done at once.

And suddenly he stopped, for he had smelled smoke. Almost silently he crept forward through the brush, and came to a small clearing.

There he saw a hut, from the chimney of which smoke was issuing. Señor Zorro circled the hut, but saw no human being. He went to the crest of the slope again, and saw a woman struggling down it toward the pirate's camp—a woman bent and old.

Señor Zorro guessed, then, that this was the hut of some aged lawbreaker no longer active in piracy. Perhaps the ancient one was down in the camp, now that the fighting was at an end, and his ancient woman was following to see the excitement.

Señor Zorro approached the hut carefully, crept around the corner of it, and peered in at the door to find the place empty. He rushed inside and sought frantically for what he desired. There came a chuckle of delight as he found it.

What he desired and found was nothing more than a ragged skirt and a wide, dirty shawl. Señor Zorro put them on quickly, bent his shoulders, and hobbled back among the trees and brush. It was a disguise that would serve for the time being.

Beneath the skirt was the sword of Zorro, ready to be whipped from its scabbard. Señor Zorro felt confident as long as the blade was at his side. He left the fringe of trees at some distance from the hut, and made his way down the slope.

As he came nearer the camp he was doubly cautious. The horses had lost some of the fright, and were grazing. The pirates, for the greater part, were gathered around the adobe building where the *caballeros* were being held prisoners. The women and children were there, too, only some of them were still scattered around the camp, looking at the dead and wounded.

Señor Zorro perceived that he had arrived at an opportune time. Nobody would give any attention to a woman stumbling along toward the scene of excitement. The pirates, undoubtedly, imagined that Zorro had ridden far away, perhaps to San Diego de Alcála for help.

He approached nearer. There were two large adobe buildings, and he supposed that the *señorita* was held prisoner in one of them, but he did not know which.

Then he stopped suddenly, and bent his shoulders more. For he saw Captain Ramón talking to Barbados, saw the *commandante* turn and leave the pirate chief and hurry into the nearest adobe building. Señor Zorro guessed that the *señorita* was there.

He hobbled forward again, alert to keep a certain distance from any of the pirates or women, for he realized that they knew one another well. He reached the corner of the building, and began to circle it, listening intently for the voice he hoped to hear.

He heard it. Pretending to be picking up something from the ground, Señor Zorro bent against the wall and listened. He heard Captain Ramón's statements, heard the *señorita* reply, listened with a grim expression on his face while the *commandante* begged for an embrace.

It would be perilous to enter that building now, Señor Zorro knew. Ramón would call the pirates, but perhaps he could be silenced first. However, there could be no hesitation. The *señorita* was there, being affronted, and was to be spared insult.

Señor Zorro saw the window, and guessed that he could manage to struggle through it. He raised his head and glanced inside. He saw the *señorita* recoiling, the *commandante* approaching her.

Señor Zorro hesitated no longer. He sprang up and scrambled through the window. He tore at the woman's clothing that clung to him, got free of it, and whipped out the sword of Zorro. He pressed the *señorita* to one side out of harm's way, and confronted his enemy.

His open hand cracked against Captain Ramón's head. And then he stepped back, on guard, giving the renegade officer his chance, though he little deserved it.

"You are alive!" the *señorita* gasped.

"Ha! Very much alive!" Señor Zorro replied. "Stand back against the wall, *señorita,* and turn your pretty face away. This is not going to be pleasant for a dainty lady's eyes to watch!"

PART FIVE

PART V

TWENTY-TWO
A PRICE TO BE PAID

THE FACE of Captain Ramón turned livid as he struggled to get his sword from its scabbard. There was a look of fear in his countenance, too.

"Zorro!" he cried. "Señor Zorro, eh?"

"*Sí!* Zorro!" came the answer. "There is not water enough in all the sea to drown me while there remains something to be avenged. We have crossed blades before, *señor*, and I have marked you. But this time shall be the last. A fatal wound this time, *capitan*! It is an honor that I do not cut you down without giving you the chance to defend yourself!"

Captain Ramón finally had his sword out, and now he was on guard. But he could not forget that once before in his life he had crossed blades with Señor Zorro, and Zorro had played with him as a cat plays with a mouse, and finally had left him for dead after marking him on the forehead.

And so the captain grew desperately afraid, feeling that he had small chance against the better sword play of the other. He sprang back toward the door to the front room, but found Señor Zorro before him blocking the way.

"Are you a coward and would run?" Zorro taunted. "A pretty soldier, by the saints!"

"Ha! Señor Zorro is here!" the *commandante* shouted at the top of his lung power. "Zorro is here! To me, pirates!"

He had no time to say more. Señor Zorro's face assumed an expression of grim determination, and he advanced swiftly. But Captain Ramón had found another method of protection for the time being. He sprang back beside the *señorita*, grasped her roughly and held her before him, shielding his body with hers. And he continued his shouting, hoping to attract the attention of Barbados and his men.

"Poltroon!" Zorro sneered. "Coward and dog!"

"Fly, Diego!" the *señorita* begged. "The pirates will be here and take you."

"When I have slain this arrant coward and rescued you, and not before!" Señor Zorro declared.

He danced toward Captain Ramón again, but the *commandante* was back in a corner now, holding the *señorita* close before him, and Señor Zorro was afraid to attempt a thrust. The *señorita* made a struggle to get free, but found that she could not.

In the other room the woman Inez had heard the tumult and the words. She had dared to open the door a crack and peer inside, and then she had closed the door again and barred it quickly, and hurried into the open.

"Barbados!" she shrieked. "Sanchez! Fiends of hell! Señor Zorro is here trying to kill the captain! Come and take him!"

Barbados heard and understood her shrieks, as did some of the others near. They rushed across the open space and crowded into the front room of the building. From the storeroom came the sound of Señor Zorro's voice.

"Hide behind a woman, eh, coward? Come out and fight, poltroon! Come out, renegade! Is there no insult strong enough to bring you forth?"

Barbados motioned with one hand. Inez unbarred the door and threw it open. Into the storeroom tumbled the pirates, their blades held ready.

"Take him alive!" Barbados thundered. "Catch me this land pirate unhurt!"

Señor Zorro whirled to confront them. He darted to a corner and threw up his blade. He sprang forward a few steps, wounded a man, retreated again.

But he knew that the weight of numbers was against him in such cramped fighting quarters, and he could not get to the window and make an escape. They hurled themselves upon him, buried him beneath their combined weight, disarmed him, and forced him to his feet again. They lashed his hands behind his back, and Barbados, now that it was a safe thing to do, stalked forward and spat at him.

"So, Señor Zorro, we have you in our hands again!" Barbados said. "This time it will be fire or steel instead of water, since you seem to swim so well! And this time, *señor*, we make a real ghost out of you!"

Captain Ramón lurched forward, his face purple with wrath. "Do with him as you will," he said to Barbados. "But let me have a hand in it!"

"Ha! You had your chance, *capitan*, a moment ago, and did not make much of it!" Barbados replied, grinning. "I'll have him put in the other adobe building with the *caballeros*. Fiends of hell, take him away!"

The *señorita* made an attempt to get forward, but the pirates thrust her back.

They took Señor Zorro away, and the grinning Barbados followed them. The captain turned to face the *señorita* once more.

"*Señorita*, you must try to understand," he said. "I could not act or speak in any other manner. The pirates must still think that I am one of them, else I cannot get to San Diego de Alcála and fetch the soldiers."

"There is small need of further pretense, *señor*," she replied with much scorn in her manner. "I know you for what you are!"

"You are inclined to show bravery, now that you know this Señor Zorro is alive, eh?" he said. "But will he live long, in the hands of these pirates, some of whose friends he has slain? This Barbados loves ransom money, but Don Diego Vega is one man who never will be ransomed. For Barbados loves vengeance, too!"

"I cannot endure your presence longer," she said. "Leave me alone with my sorrows!"

"Nor can I endure your scorn much longer," Captain Ramón replied. "Has it occurred to you that you are in my power completely, if I will it so?"

"Now you show your true colors again, *señor*. And there is always death!"

"And torture!" Captain Ramón added. "That will befall this Señor Zorro, no doubt!"

"Torture?" she cried.

"Ha! Real torture, such as only these beasts of pirates know how to inflict!" he declared. "No man can stand against such a thing for long. He will beg and shriek for the release of death when the pain begins."

"No—no!" she cried.

"And you will be forced to watch it, no doubt!" the *commandante* continued. "Barbados, his men say, is a master hand at torture of all kinds. They'll chip at him with their knives, sear his flesh with white-hot brands—"

"*Señor*, for the love of the saints—"

"You do not like the picture? Wait until you see the reality, which will be much worse than words could paint!"

"If I could save him—give my life for his—"

The captain looked at her sharply. "Perhaps there may be a way," he said.

"What mean you?"

"I can have speech with this fiend of a Barbados and coax him to delay the torture until he has accounted for the troopers from San Diego de Alcála. The troopers will account for him and his men instead, of course, and then Señor Zorro and the *caballeros* will be released."

"And you will do this?" she cried. "Ah, *señor*, if only you would!"

"I can do it, *señorita*—at a price!"

"And what—is the price?" she asked.

"You are the price yourself, *señorita.*"

"Beast!"

"Is that a way to save Señor Zorro by calling me a beast?" the captain asked. "All that I ask is an immediate marriage. Would it be an ill thing to wed with one of his excellency's officers?"

"I cannot! My heart is not my own!"

"Can you hesitate?" the captain asked. "One way, you will be my wife, and Señor Zorro will be saved from torture and will be set free. The other way, *señorita,* he will be tortured until he dies—and you will come to me unwed!"

"Oh!" she gasped. "That a man could be such a fiend—"

"Love drives men to do strange things, *señorita.*"

"Love!" she cried. "You know not the meaning of the word! To love is to be gentle, to cherish and protect!"

"I know the meaning as it appeals to me," the captain declared. "And I have scant time, if you are to agree. Fray Felipe is in the camp, and he can wed us. Barbados is afraid to affront a *fray* and will not see Felipe harmed. So he lets him roam around, though he is watched."

"I cannot!"

"Very well, *señorita.* It is for you to make the decision. But I am afraid that the pirates will have their way. And their way will not be a gentle one!"

"Can you not be a proper man?" she cried. "Can you not save him without exacting such a payment? For once in your life, *señor,* can you not show yourself a *caballero?*"

"Save him and let him claim you?" Ramón asked. "You are asking far too much!"

"Is there no other way?"

"None!" he replied. "There are certain things that you must do—be my wife, and I will save Señor Zorro by fetching the troopers from San Diego de Alcála. And afterward you must say that I did but trick the pirates, and that you wed me in gratitude for saving you from them."

"Such a falsehood would not come easily from my lips, *señor,*" she said. "And how can I trust you? How do I know that you would fetch the troopers?"

"I am not afraid to make the bargain," he told her. "You need not wed me until after the pirates are defeated and the *caballeros* are released. That is fair enough for both, is it not? But how, on the other hand, may I be assured that you will not forget your part of the bargain, once I have done my share?"

"*Señor!*" she cried, her face flaming. "Would a daughter of the Pulidos break her given word?"

"Then you give it?" he asked.

"Not yet!" she replied firmly. "There are to be certain stipulations, *señor*."

"And they—" he questioned.

"I must see Señor Zorro alone and speak to him, and explain just what I intend to do. I would tell him the truth—that you will save him and the others if I wed you. I would not have him think that my heart is one that can change so easily."

"Ha! After that you would have to save him against his will. He would not accept the sacrifice."

"Then will I save him despite himself," she declared. "And you need not fear for the future in such case, *señor*. Once we were wed, Señor Zorro would not raise his hand against you if I asked him not to do so."

"Perhaps it may be arranged," Captain Ramón said.

He was plotting more, even as he spoke. He did not see how he could lose in this game. If he fetched the troopers, and the pirates were wiped out and the *caballeros* saved, the *señorita* would keep her word if she had given it. Men might despise him for taking advantage of a situation, yet would he be safe. And perhaps, for a small sum, he could have this Señor Zorro killed yet.

And if the pirates through some fortune of war managed to be victorious over the troopers, then Captain Ramón could do the other thing—simply seize the *señorita*, give Señor Zorro up to torture, and remain a renegade, perhaps even become a pirate chief himself in the future.

"I will speak to no other man, *señor*—only Zorro," she said, as he seemed to hesitate. "I will not betray your double-dealing to the pirate crew, for that would defeat all our ends and mean death for Señor Zorro and the *caballeros*, and much worse for me. But I must speak to Señor Zorro a moment before I give you my decision in the matter."

"I will try to arrange it with Barbados," Captain Ramón replied. "Come into the other room and let the woman guard you until I return. You must play the game well if you would be successful. And there is scant time. I should start my ride to San Diego de Alcála as quickly as possible."

TWENTY-THREE
THE SEÑORITA PLOTS ALSO

CAPTAIN RAMÓN, hurrying outside, found Barbados in the open space before the other adobe building. The pirate chief, it was easy to see, had been drinking heavily of rich, stolen wine. Among the pirates slain were some of Barbados's particular friends, and he was trying to drown his sorrow at their untimely taking off.

He turned as the *commandante* approached and greeted him with a shout.

"Ha!" he cried, lurching drunkenly. "So you have not started for San Diego de Alcála yet, *capitan*? You have just come from the little *señorita—sí*? Yet your face does not bear the marks of her nails, which is strange. I would not want the taming of her. By my naked blade, I would not!"

"Attend me!" the captain commanded, grasping the pirate chief by the arm. "Is it your intention to torture this Señor Zorro your men have taken?"

Barbados cursed loudly, breathed heavily, and squinted his eyes until they were only two tiny slits. "I shall make him squirm and squeal!" he declared loudly. "And then I shall turn him into a proper ghost!"

"Death is nothing to a man like that," Captain Ramón told him. "But torture is a different matter."

"Then I'll see to it that he is prettily tortured!" Barbados declared.

"There are two sorts of torture, Barbados—the physical and the mental," said the captain.

"Mental? I do not understand such things!"

"Torture to the mind," the captain explained. "That is the worst kind by far.

If you would have some sport with this Señor Zorro, whom we both hate, listen to me. The *señorita,* who was to have been his bride, is afraid that you will torture and slay him. I have told her that I will save him by fetching the troopers from San Diego de Alcála—if she will wed with me."

"Ha! Is this treason?" Barbados cried.

"Are you a fool?" questioned the captain. "And am I one? There must be no talk of treason between us. Attend! She will go to this Señor Zorro and explain to him what she intends doing. Just think of that, Barbados! There is torture for you! He, who loves her so much, will think that she is to become the bride of another man. Ha! He will squirm and squeal indeed! A prisoner, and unable to prevent it! Ha!"

"Ha!" Barbados cried, understanding finally, and grinning to show his appreciation.

"And we will taunt him with it," the *commandante* continued. "We'll watch him squirm!"

"But it appears to me, *capitan,* that in this affair you are acting the part of an ass," Barbados dared to say. "Why work so hard to get the wench to agree to wed you when you can take her at your pleasure?"

"Because it will hurt this Señor Zorro a great deal more to know that she gives her consent," the captain replied. "We'll taunt him about it, and then I'll ride for the soldiers. And your men will sweep them off the earth and then ride to San Diego de Alcála and loot the place. As for this Señor Zorro—having tortured him mentally, you will proceed to torture him physically when you celebrate your victory."

"It appeals to me!" Barbados declared suddenly. "He slew some of my closest friends. Yet I would not wait too long! Some of these fine enemies must be tortured soon, while I am in the proper mood for it!"

"And there can be more mental torture," the captain said. "Do not touch him until the very last. Make him watch as some of his friends are being tortured. Let him hear their shrieks of pain. Let him see Don Audre Ruiz, his boon companion, suffer. That will hurt him as much as being tortured himself."

"Ha! By my naked blade, *capitan,* you should have been born a pirate!" Barbados shrieked.

"Then it is agreed?"

"*Sí!* It is agreed!"

"I will get the *señorita* and let her tell Señor Zorro what she intends to do."

"There are two rooms in that adobe building," Barbados explained. "This Señor Zorro is alone in the front one, for I thought it best not to put him with the others. The door between has a heavy lock, and I have the key. You can let the *señorita* go in there, and we'll listen at the window and enjoy his pain when she tells him. Ha! I say it again, *capitan*—you should be a pirate! You are wasted in the army!"

Captain Ramón hastened back to the *señorita,* whispered that he had been able to arrange things as she wished, grinned at old Inez, and then conducted the daughter of the Pulidos across the open space and toward the adobe building where Señor Zorro and the *caballeros* were being held prisoners.

Barbados was waiting. He leered at the girl, then called one of his men to his side, and commanded that he unfasten and open the door. Señor Zorro, his wrists still lashed behind his back, was pacing around the room. From the room adjoining came the voices of the *caballeros.*

"Señor Zorro, here is a pretty wench who has some words for your ears," Barbados called. "She is not so pretty as she was, having dirtied herself in an attempt to escape, but possibly she will serve. I give you a few minutes in which to hold speech. Do not abuse the privilege."

"Whatever you may do in the future, I thank you for this, Señor Pirate!" Zorro said.

Barbados laughed and withdrew, and closed the door behind him. The *señorita* stepped forward slowly, her hands held at her breast, a look of anguish in her sweet face. Señor Zorro was smiling down at her.

"The saints are good, *señorita*!" he whispered. "That I may see you again—"

"Diego, my beloved, it is a sad errand!" she interrupted. "Yet I had to come."

His face was grave for an instant, and then he smiled at her once more.

"So they have sent you to tell me that I must die?" he asked. "I could not receive a warrant of death from sweeter hands. My one regret is that I have failed in your rescue. I do not fear the coming of death. It will be only another adventure. It is for you that I fear."

"Fear not for me!" she said. "Nor fear the coming of death, either. It is not a warrant of death that I bring you, Diego. I have come to tell you that you are to go free."

"Free?" Señor Zorro gasped. "Have pirates turned kind? Has old Fray Felipe demonstrated to them the error of their ways? Is the devil going to mass these days? *Señorita,* you are trying to make the sentence lighter by saying it in a kind manner. Speak out! Don Diego Vega is not afraid to learn the truth, and most certainly Señor Zorro is not."

"I know that you are not afraid, Diego. I dread to tell you this thing, though it means your life."

He stepped closer to her suddenly, and looked down into her eyes. "What are you trying to tell me?" he asked kindly. "Do not be afraid to speak."

"That you are to go free, Diego," she replied, failing to meet his glance.

"And how may that be?" he asked.

"Captain Ramón is to arrange it."

"Put not your trust in Ramón!"

"Ah, Diego, but there is naught else to do!" she said. "He tells me that he is tricking the pirates. He will ride to San Diego de Alcála and return with the troopers from the *presidio* there. The pirates will be slain or captured, and you and the *caballeros* will be saved."

"Ramón will do this?" Señor Zorro cried. "Is there some hidden spark of gentlehood in the beast?"

"He will do it, Diego—for a price."

"Ha! I might have known it! Well, I can pay the cur! What is the price?"

"Not money, Diego, beloved! The price is that I wed him."

Señor Zorro sucked in his breath sharply and bent quickly over her.

"You wed with him?" he said. "Wed with a snake like Captain Ramón?"

"Only to save you, Diego! Ah, do not think that I am untrue! He but asks my word—the word of a Pulido! And the wedding is not to take place until he returns with the troopers, the pirates are slain, and you are free."

"*Señorita—*"

"There will be torture and death for you, else," she was quick to add. "And I will remain true, Diego. I shall but promise to wed him, understand. And after the ceremony, before he can claim me as his bride, I—I shall die!"

"And do you think that I would accept such a sacrifice?" Señor Zorro asked. "Could I live and see you the bride of another man? And could I live knowing that you had taken your own life for me? No, *señorita*!"

"If I do not, they will torture and slay you!"

"Then let them torture and slay!" he said. "You cannot do this thing! You—a daughter of the Pulido blood! Think of the blood in your veins!"

"I could not be his wife, except in name, but I can die!" she said. "Only a thrust of the dagger after the ceremony! The blood of the Pulidos tells me to do that!"

"I command you—entreat you—"

"Can I see you die?" she asked. "And, if I refuse, there will be nothing except death for me as well as for you. For Ramón will try, then, to make me his by force."

"Better to die in defense of your honor, *señorita,* than have your fair name linked with his even for a moment!" Señor Zorro declared. "I demand that you refuse to do this thing! Ah, *señorita,* all hope is not gone! They have taken my sword, and they have bound my hands, but I am not helpless entirely. The spirit of Zorro still burns in my breast! Given but a little time, and I'll win through!"

"Diego!"

"If we could work for time—" he said.

"Perhaps I can hold him off for an hour," she whispered. "But no longer than that, I am sure. And—there may be a way. I have thought of something!"

"What is it?"

"Whisper," she commanded. "I am sure that they are listening outside the window. Pretend that all is agreed between us. Let me embrace you!"

Barbados and Captain Ramón not only were listening, but also they were peering through the window. And they saw her go up close to him, press against him, saw her arms go around him, as though in a last embrace. But her back was toward the window, and they could not see all.

For, as she pressed against him, the little *señorita* took from her bosom the dagger that the woman Inez had given her when she had attempted to make an escape, and which had been forgotten afterward. And she reached around him even as she buried her head against his breast, and sawed with the sharp dagger at the cords that bound his wrists.

"Careful!" she warned. "Hold the ends of the ropes, so they will not know that you are free!"

"*Sí!*" he breathed. "Never in all the world was there ever a *señorita* like you! Hope sings within me again!"

"Do not let it show in your face!" she warned.

Her hands crept to the front again, and she slipped the dagger into the sash around his waist. She knew that he felt it, and knew that it was there. And then she stepped back, and raised her voice so that those at the window could hear.

"It is the only way, Diego!" she said. "I must leave you—I cannot endure this scene longer! Take my lips, Diego—for the last time!"

She raised her head, and her eyes closed. He bent forward, their lips touched. And then she gave a little cry as though of pain, and rushed back toward the door. And Señor Zorro remained standing against the wall, anguish in his countenance.

Barbados opened the door and let the *señorita* out of the room, then closed and fastened the door again. Captain Ramón hurried up to her.

"You have decided, *señorita*?" he asked.

"Almost am I ready to give you my sacred word, but not quite," she replied. "It is a terrible thing for me, *señor*. Give me but one little hour. Let me go to old Fray Felipe and have him pray with me."

"I am growing tired of waiting!" Captain Ramón said. "I should be on my way already. Why not decide now?"

"You will have ample time to return with the troopers long before nightfall," she whispered quickly, as Barbados turned away to howl an order to some of his men. "Give me only an hour—perhaps less!"

"Very well—an hour!" said the captain. "But no longer! I'll find the *fray* for you, and put you both in one of the huts under guard until you can make up your mind."

TWENTY-FOUR
INTO THE OPEN

SEÑOR ZORRO FOUGHT the battle of his life, after the little *señorita* had gone and the door had been closed and barred, to keep from showing his elation in his face.

His hands now would be free at any time he wished to drop the ends of the cords that bound his wrists. He had a weapon hidden in the sash about his waist. Given those minor advantages, Señor Zorro felt that he could disconcert his enemies again, else fail to be Zorro.

But the expression in his face did not change as he walked slowly around the room and finally came to a stop before the window and glanced across the clearing and the beach toward the glistening water of the bay. He looked like a man devoid of all hope, expecting the worst.

Not so very far away was a small hut, before the one door of which two of the pirates sat on guard. Señor Zorro was well aware of the fact that the weapons of the captured *caballeros*, and those of their comrades who had been slain, were in there, and that his own beloved sword was there also, waiting to be claimed by him.

And, as he watched, Sanchez rode wildly into the clearing on a magnificent horse, undoubtedly stolen from some great *hacienda*. Barbados's lieutenant dismounted and allowed the animal to wander near the hut while he hurried in search of the pirate chief with some report.

These things Señor Zorro saw quickly, and then he hurried back to the door that opened into the other room. It was barred, and locked with a strong lock, and Zorro had no tools with which to open it. He could not unfasten it and release his friends, but he could hold speech with them.

He made certain that nobody was near the window to overhear, and then kicked against the door to attract the attention of the *caballeros*.

"Audre!" he called, in a guarded voice.

There was silence for a moment, and then he heard a whisper from the other side of the door.

"*Sí?*"

"I have another chance, Audre. The *señorita* has cut my bonds and given me a dagger. It is a poor weapon, but better than none. It would avail us nothing for me to let you out if I could, for the pirates greatly outnumber us. But I can try to escape and ride to San Diego de Alcála for troopers."

"Good, Diego, my friend!"

"I know not what may happen before I am able to return. Ramón is in the camp and up to some sort of deviltry. But, should you escape, look to the *señorita*!"

"Be assured of that!" Don Audre replied.

"If I can do so, when I escape I'll take her with me. If not, I'll return with the troopers as swiftly as possible. The saints be with you!"

"And with you!" Don Audre Ruiz returned.

Señor Zorro walked slowly away from the door and approached the window again. The horse Sanchez had been riding was now but a short distance from the adobe building. The two guards were squatted before the hut wherein the captured weapons had been stored, drinking and talking. Other pirates were in the distance, walking around, stretched in the shade of the huts, gambling, shouting, quarreling.

Señor Zorro knew well that it would profit nothing to get those weapons in the hut, for the *caballeros* could not be liberated quickly, and so the element of surprise in an attack would be lost. Moreover, were they liberated and their swords in their hands, they would only be cut down by the pirate crew after they had taken some toll.

Señor Zorro wanted his own sword, but did not know whether there would be time for him to get possession of it. He would not dare stop to attack the two guards, for the other pirates would rush up and endanger his chance for escape. It would be far better, he decided quickly, to seize the horse and ride with what speed he could toward the distant village of San Diego de Alcála, get help there at the *presidio*, and return to the work of rescue with an armed force behind him.

Back to the door he hurried.

"Audre!" he called, softly.

"Sí?"

"Raise a din in there, create a bedlam of a sort, and 'twill help me vastly. Pretend to be fighting among yourselves."

He did not have very long to wait. He could hear Don Audre Ruiz whispering instructions to the other *caballeros,* and almost instantly they began shrieking at one another, pounding on the heavy door, making a bedlam of noise. Señor Zorro hurried across to the outside window and called to the guards before the hut.

"Come here!" he shouted. "The prisoners are fighting and slaying one another!"

But they refused to leave their posts, as Señor Zorro had hoped they would do. Instead, they shrieked the news at Barbados, who was not far away, and he ran toward the adobe building followed by Sanchez and half a dozen of the men. They unbarred the door and burst in upon Señor Zorro, who stood back against the wall gazing at the door of the adjoining room, as though trying to decide what was taking place inside. From the other side of that door came shrieks and cries and the sounds of blows.

"Fiends of hell!" Barbados swore. "They will slay one another, and then there will be neither torture nor ransom! Unfasten that door and stand ready to drive them back if they try to make an escape. And two of you guard that outside door also!"

One glance he flung at Señor Zorro, to find him standing against the wall as if his attention were concentrated on the other room. But as Barbados turned toward the door again Señor Zorro shifted along the wall for a distance of a few feet, and glanced toward the door through which he would have to go to freedom.

He waited until the other door was about to be thrown open, until the pirates in the room had their attention centered there, and then Señor Zorro dropped the severed cords from his wrists, wriggled his fingers for an instant to restore the circulation of blood, and suddenly brought his hands around in front of him and tore the dagger from his sash, where the little *señorita* had put it.

Forward he hurled himself, just as the other door was opened. He took the two men before him by surprise. One he hurled aside; the other he was forced to wound slightly to get him out of the way. Past them he dashed, even as they shrieked the intelligence that he was escaping. Out into the open he darted and straight toward the horse that Sanchez had ridden into the clearing. He would have no difficulty in getting to the horse, he saw. But his escape was all that he could negotiate. A glance told him that the *señorita* was not in sight, and he had no time to search the entire camp for her.

The pirates were rushing toward him from every side, attracted by the tumult. Barbados, behind him, was shrieking commands and foul oaths. The dagger held between his teeth, Señor Zorro dodged the two men before the hut and vaulted into the saddle, kicked at the animal's flanks, and was away.

Behind him a pistol barked, but the ball flew wild, and he could hear the insane roar of rage that Barbados gave because he had missed the target. It was a flying target now. Señor Zorro bent low over the horse's neck and kicked frantically at the animal's flanks again. Straight across the clearing he guided the animal, toward the trail that ran to the crest of the slope.

Another pistol roared behind him, but he did not even hear the shrill whistling of the flying ball. He wished that he might make a search for the *señorita*, but he was afraid that capture might result if he tried it. And were he captured again Barbados would make short work of him. It were better to get away free and return later to rescue.

He was approaching the edge of the camp now. He knew that there were some mounts with saddles and bridles on, and that there might be a pursuit. Once over the crest, he would have a chance. The pirates would not dare follow him too close to San Diego de Alcála, and that was only eight miles away.

And then he saw, just ahead of him, Captain Ramón. The *commandante* was drinking from a bottle and talking to some women of the camp. He whirled around when he heard the mad pounding of the horse's hoofs, and Señor Zorro saw his face go white as he struggled to get his sword from its scabbard. The *commandante* had recognized him.

The women shrieked and fled. Captain Ramón, his sword out, stood his ground. Straight toward him Señor Zorro raced his horse, bending forward, his dagger held in his right hand again. Now he wished he had his beloved sword!

But Ramón sprang out of the way just in time and swung his blade in a vicious blow. It missed Señor Zorro and struck the horse on the rump, inflicting a minor cut. It had the effect, however, of frightening the animal more. Up the slope he raced, and Señor Zorro sat straight in the saddle and shrieked at the top of his voice:

"*Atención!* A *caballero's* near—"

It was not merely in a spirit of bravado. It was to let the little *señorita* know, if she did not already, that he was free and riding wildly for help.

TWENTY-FIVE
AT THE PRESIDIO

IN THAT INSTANT, as he watched the singing Zorro racing up the slope toward the crest, Captain Ramón realized that his future was hanging by a very thin thread. Were he to protect his own interests he must move swiftly.

He sensed that Señor Zorro would make a mad ride for San Diego de Alcála and pour a story into the ear of the *commandante* of the *presidio* there. And it was highly imperative that Captain Ramón tell a far better story—and tell it first.

Ramón managed to return his sword to its scabbard, and then he raced with what speed he could toward Barbados and the others, who were following lurchingly in Señor Zorro's wake. He grasped Barbados by an arm and hurried him aside.

"What happened?" the *commandante* demanded.

"The fellow tricked us in some fashion!" Barbados declared with an oath. "His hands were untied, and he had a dagger. If that pretty wench we let speak with him—"

"Attend me!" Ramón cried. "The wench is under guard in one of the huts, and is not to be touched. Get me a horse. Be quick about it! The fool is riding to San Diego for troopers!"

"Ha! Let them come!"

"I must get to the *presidio* before he arrives," Captain Ramón explained. "The lieutenant there will take orders from me. Then I'll lead the troopers into your ambush, as we had planned. And this Zorro—"

"Ha! This Zorro!" Barbados cried. "When I have my hands upon him again there'll be no delay."

"I'll have him imprisoned in the *presidio*," the captain promised. "Then, after you defeat the soldiers, and when you go to loot the town, he will be at your mercy."

"You think of everything!" Barbados declared. "I say it yet once again—you should be a pirate!"

One of the men, understanding more than his fellows, had fetched the captain's own horse, with saddle and bridle on. The captain sprang into the saddle.

"Arrange the ambush at the head of the cañon, as we planned," he told Barbados. "Do it without delay. I'll lead the troopers straight into the trap."

Then he touched spurs to the animal he bestrode and dashed up the slope in the wake of Señor Zorro.

Captain Ramón was an excellent horseman, and he rode an excellent mount. Moreover, he had been through every mile of that country with his troopers some time before. He knew the shortest route to the *presidio* at San Diego de Alcála, and he felt quite sure that Señor Zorro did not.

Reaching the crest of the slope, Captain Ramón stopped his horse beneath the trees and watched and listened for a time. From the distance there came to his ears the drumming of a horse's hoofs. As he had expected, Señor Zorro had ridden along the bottom of the cañon, and Captain Ramón knew that such a course would take him at least two miles out of his way. Once in that cañon, a horseman was forced to follow it until he came to the other end.

Captain Ramón turned his horse's head in another direction and drove home the spurs. He rode around a hill and emerged upon a flat space, across which he raced toward a row of foothills in the distance. Señor Zorro had the start, but he was taking the long way. Aside from an accident, Captain Ramón could reach San Diego de Alcála and have his story told before Señor Zorro arrived.

The thing had to be done, he told himself. He would use his authority and have Zorro thrown into the guardroom at the *presidio*. He would go back to the pirate camp at the head of the troopers, see that the pirates were wiped out to a man, release the *caballeros* and the *señorita*.

And then there would be other things to do. He would convince the authorities that Señor Zorro had been allied with the pirates and that the *caballeros* had not known of it, and have Zorro hanged. He would ask his friend, the Governor, to order the *señorita* to wed with him because he had saved her and wiped out the pirate brood, and the *señorita* would be forced to obey his excellency's command. And he would see to it that all men believed he had been true and loyal continually.

If the *señorita* spoke out the truth Captain Ramón could smile and say she uttered a falsehood because she did not wish to wed with him. He was guarded against every emergency, he felt.

There was a mere possibility, of course, that the pirates might be victorious, and in such case Captain Ramón would pretend that he had been with the rogues always, turn pirate himself, and have the *señorita*. But he preferred the other way.

He thought of these things as he rode. Around another hill and down a slope he rushed, and when he came to a wide trail that ran toward the distant El Camino Real he knew that he had distanced Señor Zorro. Yet he rode furiously, for he wanted all the time he could have at the *presidio* before Zorro arrived.

And finally he reached the highway, and tore along it like a mad horseman riding on the wind. The mount beneath him was showing signs of wearying, but the captain urged him on. Now he was flying past natives' huts scattered along the broad highway. Children and chickens and swine hurried from his path. Women came to the doors of the huts to look after him through clouds of dust.

Then he could see, in the distance, the *presidio* on its little hill, and the group of buildings around it. Captain Ramón urged his horse cruelly. As he approached men turned to watch him. Before the *presidio* itself troopers sprang to their feet, as men will when there is a feeling of excitement in the air.

Captain Ramón stopped his horse in a cloud of dust before the *presidio* entrance and was out of the saddle before the nearest trooper could seize the bridle. The men saluted, but Captain Ramón spent no time in answering their salutes. Drawing off his gloves, he strode through the entrance and straight toward the office of the *commandante*.

He had lied nobly to Barbados. Instead of their being a smaller force of soldiers than usual at San Diego de Alcála, there was an extra detachment, come to relieve others who were to go toward the north. But only a lieutenant was there by way of officer, the real *commandante* being on a journey to San Francisco de Asis to explain certain things to the Governor.

Captain Ramón opened the office door and strode inside, gasping his breath, slapping the dust from his uniform. The lieutenant sprang to his feet.

"Ramón!" he cried. "So far from home—"

Captain Ramón stopped him with a gesture.

"Have your trumpeter sound the assembly, and gather your men while we talk!" he commanded. "This is serious—and urgent!"

The lieutenant was a good soldier, and did not question. He sprang to the door and called an order, and almost immediately the commanding notes of a trumpet rang through the place. Then the lieutenant closed the door and hurried back to the long table in the middle of the room, before which Ramón was sitting.

"Pirates within eight miles of you!" Ramón declared. "They have a large camp. Three nights ago they raided Reina de Los Angeles."

"The news has reached us."

"Ha! I followed by land and approached their rendezvous at an early hour this morning. They abducted Señorita Lolita Pulido. Some *caballeros* pursued them by sea, fought, and were overcome. Many are being held prisoners, for ransom and torture. The *señorita* is a prisoner also."

"Where?" the lieutenant asked.

"On the coast, a bit north. I lurked about the camp and made some discoveries. Señor Zorro is mixed up with them."

"Zorro?" the lieutenant gasped.

"The same. His wild blood has broken out again. The *señorita* is of the opinion that he followed to rescue her, when in reality he had her stolen. He was to have married her, but is eager for lawlessness, it appears. This will be the end of the fiend!"

"Ha!" the lieutenant gasped. "If—"

"Attend!" Ramón interrupted. "I overheard a plot. Zorro is to ride here wildly and tell of the *señorita* and the *caballeros* being held by the pirates. It is his intention to lead back the troopers—and lead them into an ambush."

"By the saints—"

"So the pirates will wipe out your men. And then San Diego de Alcála, unprotected, will be before him!"

"The fiend!" the lieutenant gasped.

"Call half a dozen of your trusted men and have them ready. When he enters and begins his story have him seized. Throw him into the guardroom and put him into the maniac's shirt. Then I'll help you lead the troopers. I know how the ambush is planned. We'll attack in the rear, save the *caballeros,* and rescue the *señorita*—and gain considerable credit. Promotion will come to you!"

"It is agreed!" the lieutenant said, his face beaming.

"Be quick about it. I'll disappear while Zorro tells his tale. Seize him, throw him into the guardroom, put him into the maniac's shirt, leave two men to guard him. When we return we'll see that he is punished for his perfidy. *Caballero* or not, he'll be hanged for this."

The lieutenant sprang from his chair to issue the necessary orders. But the door was hurled open—and Señor Zorro rushed into the officer's room!

TWENTY-SIX
HELPLESSNESS

ON THE OCCASION of this meeting it was Señor Zorro who was properly astonished instead of his foe. Captain Ramón had been the last person he had seen at the pirates' camp; he had ridden at great speed, and yet here was the *commandante* ahead of him at the *presidio* in San Diego de Alcála.

But it did not take Señor Zorro long to guess that the captain had taken advantage of some short cut across the country and so had arrived at the *presidio* first. And, since he was here, Señor Zorro found himself in something of a predicament.

For weapons he had only the short dagger and his courage. The element of surprise upon which he generally depended so much was acting against him instead of for him in this present encounter; but he did not despair.

He took two quick steps forward, and the dagger suddenly was in his right hand. He glanced quickly at the lieutenant, who had picked up his sword from the long table and was drawing it from the scabbard, and then whirled toward Captain Ramón, who already had his sword ready for use.

"So!" Señor Zorro cried. "You got here ahead of me, did you? Renegade and traitor!"

"'Tis you who are the renegade and traitor!" Captain Ramón declared. "Friend of pirates!"

"Ha! So that is the tale you have told?" Señor Zorro gasped. "Lieutenant, I am Don Diego Vega, of Reina de Los Angeles. Perhaps you have heard the name?"

"The lieutenant also has heard of Señor Zorro, and knows that he and Don

Diego Vega are one and the same man," Captain Ramón said before the other officer could reply. Captain Ramón felt some small degree of courage now, since Señor Zorro had no weapon except his short dagger.

"Ha! Who has not heard of Zorro?" came the reply. "And it is not to be expected that one of his excellency's officers would go far out of his regular way to do Señor Zorro a service. Yet an officer will serve his duty, and there are certain things to be considered, lieutenant. In a pirate camp a few miles from this place is a *señorita* of proper blood and several *caballeros* who must be rescued before they are tortured. I have ridden here for help, having made an escape."

"Made your escape?" Captain Ramón cried. "You came purposely with the story to lead the soldiers into a trap, you mean. Your story will avail you nothing, Señor Zorro. The lieutenant already is planning to ride to the rescue of his men. But you will remain here, a prisoner in the guardroom, in a maniac's shirt—"

"Ha!" Señor Zorro shrieked. "Lieutenant, make no mistake about it. This Captain Ramón may outrank you, but he is a traitor, and I would have all honest men know it. He is in league with the pirates himself."

"You scarcely can expect me to believe that," the lieutenant replied, smiling.

"It is the truth, by the saints! He is planning to lead your men into an ambush, no doubt!"

"I think that we have had enough of this nonsense, Don Diego!" the lieutenant said, his official manner upon him.

"You believe Captain Ramón in preference to me?"

"I do! You are to consider yourself a prisoner, Don Diego. You'll be held here safe until the rescue has been accomplished, and then there will be an investigation of this entire affair."

"It will not be necessary for you to keep me a prisoner," Señor Zorro replied, his eyes narrowing. "Lead your own soldiers, as you will, and be quick about it, and do not listen to the advice of Captain Ramón. The *señorita* who is held a captive is my betrothed. Her name is Lolita Pulido. At least allow me to remain free to aid in her rescue."

"I cannot forget that you are Señor Zorro as well as Don Diego Vega, and that the Pulido family does not have the friendship of the Governor," the lieutenant answered. "Captain Ramón has preferred a charge against you also. You remain in the *presidio* a prisoner."

The lieutenant picked up a silver whistle from the table, and started to put it to his lips to blow a blast that would call his orderly. But Señor Zorro, it appeared, had no intention of being kept a prisoner. He glanced swiftly toward Captain Ramón again, and then darted forward.

The lieutenant's whistle was knocked from his left hand, but Señor Zorro did not succeed in getting possession of the officer's sword as he hurled him aside. He dashed on to the wall, struck it and whirled away, and came back with considerable momentum. Captain Ramón had started toward the door.

But as he put out a hand to pull the door open Señor Zorro grasped a small stool that stood at one end of the long table and hurled it with precise aim. It struck the captain's arm and caused him to recoil with a cry of pain.

The lieutenant was young, and enjoyed the recklessness of his youth. He bellowed his challenge and charged. Señor Zorro caught his sword against the dagger and warded off the blow. But, to do so, he was compelled to give some ground, and so Captain Ramón got to the door and opened it.

"Troopers!" he cried. "Help! This way! Your *commandante* is attacked!"

Señor Zorro fenced the lieutenant for a moment, but he knew well that he could not do so for long with any great degree of success. And suddenly he dropped to his knees, and the lieutenant, lunging with his blade, tripped over him and sprawled on the floor. Zorro was upon his feet again before Captain Ramón could reach his side. Again he whirled, and Captain Ramón recoiled against the wall, his sword advanced, his left arm stretched out across a wood panel.

Señor Zorro did not care to encounter the long blade with his dagger; besides, he heard the soldiers coming. His arm flashed, and the dagger flew through the air. Through the sleeve of Captain Ramón's uniform coat went the sharp blade, to be driven almost to the hilt in the wood beyond. The captain was held safely for the moment.

There was one large window in the officer's room, and it was swinging open. Zorro dashed for it, reached it, sprang up as the wondering troopers rushed in through the door. Through the window Señor Zorro plunged, sprawled on the ground for an instant, and then was upon his feet again and running with renewed vigor toward the front of the building.

But disaster waited for him there. The horse he had ridden had been jaded, and a soldier had taken the mount to the rear to rub it down. Zorro found his horse gone, and that of Captain Ramón also. The troopers in front of the *presidio* were in their saddles. And they surrounded the unmounted horses of those who had rushed inside in answer to the captain's call.

Señor Zorro turned immediately to flee. But the shrieks from inside the *presidio* told the troopers what was happening. They forced their mounts forward, ran Señor Zorro down, cut off his flight, and surrounded him. For a moment there was a pretty battle; but the troopers did not strike to slay, not understanding, quite, the status of this man who seemed to have run amuck. However, they prevented an escape.

The lieutenant shrieked from the window, demanding an immediate capture. Señor Zorro made one last attempt to escape. He darted beneath the belly of a horse, got outside the circle of troopers, and dashed away. He reached the corner of the low building and went up it as a fly goes up a wall, using the rough masonry of the corner as stepping-stones.

Across the roof he darted, while the soldiers urged their horses forward again in an effort to surround the building. Down the other side of the roof he ran, skipping across the Spanish tiles until he reached the eaves.

Below him was his horse, and the hostler was wiping one of the animal's forelegs. Señor Zorro did not hesitate. He crouched and sprang, and landed in the saddle. The hostler rolled to one side in fright as the animal lurched forward.

Señor Zorro whirled the beast toward the highway. But he saw at a glance that there was small chance of escape. The mount he bestrode was almost exhausted, and the troopers had fresh mounts. And they were upon him with a rush.

Weaponless, he could do nothing. They charged around him, pulled him down from the saddle, made him prisoner, and then marched him back to the entrance of the *presidio*, where the lieutenant and Captain Ramón were waiting.

"The maniac's shirt for him!" the lieutenant commanded. "Put him into it and then into the guardroom. Two men will remain behind to see that he does not escape. But I scarcely think that even Señor Zorro can escape the maniac's shirt!"

"Put me in it, and I hold it against you!" Zorro warned.

"I have given my orders," the lieutenant replied loftily.

"One last word for your ear!" Zorro said. "You are making a sad mistake. I tell you here and now, before some of your men, that this Captain Ramón is a renegade and a traitor. Heed not his advice! And ride swiftly, else you'll not accomplish the rescue. I charge you to take the *señorita* to a place of safety."

"Certainly, *señor*!"

"You'll not let me ride with you?"

"I have given my orders."

"Lieutenant, I swear by my honor as a *caballero* that all I have told you is the truth. Does that carry weight with you?"

It seemed to carry weight, for the officer hesitated. A *caballero* does not pledge his honor lightly. But how could it be possible that an officer like Captain Ramón could be anything but loyal and true. And Captain Ramón himself decided the lieutenant.

"For a *caballero* to swear by his honor is a great thing," the captain said. "Yet now and then we find a man of *caballero* blood who forgets the honor that should be his. And we remember that you are Señor Zorro, also!"

"*Señor*—" Zorro began angrily.

But the lieutenant cut him short. "I have decided," he said. "You will be held a prisoner in the maniac's shirt until we return. Take him away!"

The soldiers grasped him roughly, hurried him inside and to the guard-room. There, Señor Zorro tried to fight again, but could accomplish nothing against so many foes. They lashed his ankles and knees and tied his wrists together in front of him. And then one fetched the maniac's shirt. The latter was exactly what it was named, an instrument used on violent maniacs to prevent them harming themselves or anybody else. It was a long bag of leather, constructed so that a man could be slipped into it bound, and the top of the bag then gathered around his neck with a leather thong.

Protesting to the last, Señor Zorro was put inside the leather bag and the neck thong tightened. And then they propped him up on a bench in a corner, and left the room. The door closed; he heard the bar go up against it.

The soldiers hurried away. There was a moment of silence. And then Señor Zorro heard the clattering of horses' hoofs as they rode toward the highway. And he was left behind, bound and helpless, in the guardroom of the *presidio*, in the maniac's shirt, and with two troopers just outside the door.

PART SIX

PART VI

TWENTY-SEVEN
FRAY FELIPE USES HIS WIT

BARBADOS, who had been drinking heavily of the rich, stolen wine since the culmination of the fight with the *caballeros* and the crew of the trading schooner, had reached the stage where he was surly, mean, dangerous. The sensational escape of Señor Zorro had been as oil poured upon flames with the pirate chief. He roared and cursed like a fiend after Captain Ramón had ridden away in pursuit, cuffed some of his men out of the way, and then stood with his fists planted against his hips, his feet wide apart, a black look in his face, his tiny eyes glittering ominously as he glanced toward the adobe building wherein the *caballero* prisoners were quartered.

Sanchez and the others who knew Barbados best had been busy keeping out of his way and so escaping trouble, but now Barbados bellowed loudly for his lieutenant, and Sanchez was forced to disclose himself. He approached his chief warily, ready to turn and run if Barbados was in a belligerent mood; but he saw at a glance that what wrath Barbados was enjoying was not directed toward his second in command.

"Sanchez! Fiend of the fiends!" he shouted. "By my naked blade, it is in my mind that we are growing weary because of the lack of sport."

"Then we must have sport," Sanchez said. "If you've anything to suggest—"

"We have prisoners," Barbados remarked, licking his thick lips, "and it is possible that a little torture would not be amiss. Say, roasting at the stake for one of those high-born *caballeros* whose blood is gentle."

"Ha!" Sanchez grunted. "It is an excellent idea—if we draw out the man's agony."

"The drawing out of his agony can be accomplished without a great deal of trouble," Barbados declared. "We'll make him squirm and squeal."

"But there is an ambush to be prepared for the soldiers," Sanchez suggested.

"There will be ample time for that at a later hour," replied the pirate chief. "It will take some time for those troopers to gallop out here from San Diego de Alcála. We can fight better if we have more wine to drink and some sort of sport to watch before giving battle."

"And which of the *caballeros* shall be roasted?" Sanchez wanted to know. "All of them are valuable men from the standpoint of ransom."

"Ha! One can be spared," said Barbados. "Not a man in that adobe but has very rich relatives. What sum we lose from the one we roast we can fasten on the others. We'll force them to gamble and decide the victim themselves. That is a happy thought. Come with me and fetch half a dozen trusted men along."

Barbados, having arrived at a decision, started straight for the adobe building as Sanchez shouted to some of the men nearest. The pirate chief unfastened the outer door and entered with the others at his heels. Then he unlocked the inner door and threw it open.

The *caballeros* were sprawled around the room, talking to one another in low tones, and they turned and looked at Barbados as he stood before them, much as men might have looked at an intruder. Scorn was in every face, and the pirate chief was quick to notice it.

"So you raised a din and attracted our attention, and thus aided this Señor Zorro to escape!" Barbados accused. "It is in my mind that there must be some punishment for that."

The *caballeros* turned from him again and began talking to one another once more as though Barbados had not addressed them. He growled a curse low down in his throat and took another step toward them, glaring ferociously.

"I have here a pack of cards properly shuffled," Barbados said, his glare changing to a fiendish grin. "I'll put them on this bench, and you prisoners will form into a line, walk past the bench, and each draw a card. The man who draws the first deuce will be the victim."

"Victim of what?" one asked.

"Of torture!" Barbados roared. "The stake! Roasting! My men demand sport, and I am the one to give it to them. It is an even thing for you—the gods of chance will decide."

"And suppose, *señor*," said Don Audre Ruiz, stepping forward with a great deal of sarcasm and scorn in his manner, "that we do not care to play your game?"

"Ha! The solution of the difficulty is easy if you do not," Barbados assured him. "In such case, since you seem to be the leader here, we'll torture you and thereafter two others picked out at random."

"Death is close behind you, pirate, if you do this thing!" Don Audre warned.

"But you will not be here to see it if you are roasted first," the pirate chief reminded him. "Line up, prisoners! Do *caballeros* shake with fear at such a time?"

Don Audre Ruiz took another step forward and sneered in the face of Barbados. "*Caballeros* are not aware of the existence of such a thing as fear!" he declared. "If there is no other way, put down your pack of cards. But if you have courage and the spirit of fair play, let me fight it out with any two of your crew of fiends—a dagger against long blades."

"Do I resemble a fool?" Barbados requested to know. "Have I but half a mind? Run a needless chance when we have you powerless already? Ha! A *caballero* might do such a fool thing, but I am not a *caballero*."

"A blind man could see that," Don Audre retorted.

"Ha! More of your insults and I'll roast the lot of you! Line up! Here are the cards."

Barbados put the greasy pack down on the end of the bench and stood back, folding his great arms across his chest. Don Audre Ruiz glanced around at his comrades, and they began forming the line. Sergeant Gonzales, feeling a bit out of place, dropped back to the end. And then the line moved forward, and the first man turned a card and saw that it was a ten, and passed on.

One by one they advanced to the bench, picked up a card, showed it to Barbados, and moved forward again, playing with death, but with inscrutable faces.

"Ha!" the pirate chief cried. "Fortunate *caballeros*, eh? But one of you must draw a deuce soon. And then my men will have rare sport. We'll see whether a *caballero* of gentle blood will squeal and squirm when the hot flames lick at him. We'll let the women torment him first, and the children! Well— Ha!"

Barbados suddenly bent forward, an evil smile upon his face. Don Audre had reached the bench and had turned over his card—the deuce of spades!

Don Audre drew in his breath sharply, but his face gave never a sign of emotion. The others crowded forward.

"Ha!" Barbados shrieked. "It is well done and appropriate! You are their leader, *señor*, and possibly will set them an example how to die. For you we will make the fire hotter and the torment longer. We'll see how long you can live."

"He'll flinch quick enough!" Sanchez cried, grinning.

Don Audre Ruiz tossed the card away and dusted his hands as though the bit of pasteboard had soiled them. Then he raised his head proudly and looked Barbados straight in the eyes.

"How soon?" Don Audre Ruiz asked.

"How soon, *caballero*? Now, at once, and immediately! My men crave sport!" Barbados cried. "And while they listen to your shrieks and pleas for mercy they can drink some rich wine we took from Reina de Los Angeles."

"Are you human man enough to let me have speech with Fray Felipe before I die?" Don Audre asked.

"Want to pray with him, do you?" Barbados sneered. "I'll have him at the stake for you. You can pray through the smoke."

There was a sudden jostling in the crowd, and Sergeant Gonzales shouldered his way to the front.

"Foul pirate!" said he. "Murderer and fiend, let me make a deal!"

"What is this?" Barbados asked.

"I am a bigger man than the *caballero* here, and fatter men roast better. Also, I wear the uniform of the Governor, and you hate such uniforms. I'm twice the coward that Don Ruiz is. I'd squirm and squeal twice as much. Ha! Would it not be better sport to roast me at the stake?"

"You want to die for him?" Barbados asked.

"I offer myself in his place, since your fiends must be amused. I did not get a chance to draw a card, or surely I'd have drawn a deuce."

Don Audre put his hand on the sergeant's arm.

"This is useless, my friend," he said.

"Not so!" Sergeant Gonzales declared. "You are a fine man of parts, Don Audre Ruiz, and really amount to something in the world. And I am but a big pig. There are many better men who can fill my place."

"Whatever your birth and station, you are now, in my estimation, a *caballero* and a brave man," Don Audre said.

Barbados roared his laughter.

"A hero!" he sneered. "I cannot let you take the *caballero's* place, fool soldier, but, since you wish to be roasted, your wish is granted. We'll roast you later, when we have need of more sport. These other *caballeros* will be ransomed, but there is nobody in the world who would ransom you for as much as a bottle of thin wine."

"That is true, fiend of hell!" Sergeant Gonzales said.

"But it is not true!" Don Audre Ruiz cried, his face lighting. He whirled to confront the other *caballeros*. "Friends, promise me this last request—have your people make up a purse and ransom this soldier," he said. "He has been the friend of Don Diego Vega for years. We used to smile at that peculiar friendship, but now I can understand. The sergeant, also, is a man of parts, and Don Diego realized it while we were blind. A last handshake, and then—"

They surged toward him, and Barbados and his men stepped back to the door and waited. There was an evil grin on the face of the pirate chief again. The gods of chance were working in his favor, he felt, when they had delivered this *caballero* into his hands for his evil purposes.

"Come, *señor*!" he ordered. "It is not gentlemanly to keep my men waiting long for their fun."

Don Audre Ruiz shook the hands of his friends for the last time and turned away. They led him out and closed and barred the door again. They conducted him through the front room and into the open, first binding his hands behind his back.

"If you are a human being, let me see Fray Felipe," Don Audre said.

"I'll have him beside the stake," Barbados promised. "He can mumble over you all he likes."

Some of the pirates were shouting the news of what was to occur. Men came running from every direction, shouting and laughing and waving bottles, determined to see how a *caballero* could die. Women and children hurried from their huts.

The stake was ready, for it often had been used before, both for prisoners and pirates. It was a favorite method Barbados had of punishing traitors and those he deemed guilty of breaking some of the many laws he laid down. It stood near the sea, a long metal bar upright in the soil, the débris of many fires scattered around it and half buried in the shifting sand.

Already some of the men were hurrying toward the stake with fuel. The women and children were shrieking insults at the condemned man. But Don Audre Ruiz held his head proudly, and his lips were curled in scorn. Only the unusual pallor in his face told that there was a tumult of emotions within his breast.

They lashed him to the stake and made his body fast there with ropes and leather thongs. One chain they wrapped around him to hold him fast after the ropes had been burned away. Women spat at him, children hurled at him small stones and scoops of sand. The pirates danced around him like savages, waving wine bottles and brandishing their cutlasses.

"So you think that you will not squirm and squeal, eh?" Barbados taunted. "In a very few minutes we'll learn the truth concerning that."

"You promised me the *fray*," Don Audre Ruiz replied. "But I did not think that a pirate could keep his given word."

"Ha! I'll show you that I can play at having gentle blood!" Barbados laughed. "Matter of honor, eh? The *fray*! Fetch me the old *fray*, some of you!"

The dancing and drinking was continued, and more fuel was heaped around the stake and its victim. A few feet distant stood a man with a flaming torch. Barbados, his arms folded across his chest, stood waiting to give the word. And after a time old Fray Felipe thrust his way among them and reached the side of the pirate chief.

"What is this that you would do?" he demanded.

"We intend to broil this *caballero* until he is done properly," Barbados replied. "Being a pious soul, he has need of a priest before he dies. So we have sent for you."

Fray Felipe knew that there was small chance for an argument here. Ordinarily Barbados was exceedingly superstitious where a man of the church was concerned, but now wine had given him a false courage. If Fray Felipe saved Don Audre Ruiz now it would not be through an appeal to the heart of Barbados.

And so Fray Felipe did a peculiar thing—a thing that startled them all, and Don Audre most of all. He threw back his gray head and laughed.

Barbados blinked his eyes rapidly, and Sanchez swore softly beneath his breath. Had the *fray* gone insane suddenly? Were his wits wandering? It was a horrible thing to see an old *fray* laugh like that.

"So it is as I suspected," Fray Felipe declared. "I had thought for a moment, Barbados, that you were a pirate leader in truth, a general with brains. But you play the boy."

"How is this?" Barbados cried.

"Traitors play with you, and you walk into traps. You and your fiends spend time at such cruel sports as this while your enemies are preparing to annihilate you—"

"*Fray*, what is your meaning?"

"Are you blind?" Fray Felipe asked. "Are you an utter and simple fool? You have put your confidence and trust in this Captain Ramón. And at this moment he is riding back from San Diego de Alcála at the head of the troopers, perhaps."

"Ha! I know it, *fray*. He is leading the soldiers into an ambush!"

"So you are such an easy dupe!" Fray Felipe said. "I know his plans, and so does the little *señorita*. You will form your ambush at the head of the cañon. And he will lead the troopers around it, attack you in the rear, cut you off from your camp, and annihilate you. By doing that he'll save his face and gain favor with decent men and women and with the Governor. He'll claim that he saved the *señorita*, and ask her in marriage, get her for a bride without cutting himself off forever from honest men. A man who can be traitor to one cause, Señor Pirate, can be traitor to another."

"Lies!" Barbados thundered.

"They are not lies!" Fray Felipe declared. "And you are playing here when you should be preparing for the battle. Easy victims you'll be for the troopers!"

Barbados seemed to hesitate. There was a quality in the *fray's* words and bearing that indicated truth. Then there came a woman's screech, and Inez thrust herself forward.

"The old *fray* speaks the truth!" she declared. "I overheard the *commandante* talking to the *señorita*. He told her that he was tricking you."

"By my naked blade!" Barbados swore.

"He is doubly a traitor!" the woman screeched. "I would not trust him. Make ready to fight the soldiers. Do not be caught in a trap. The man at the stake can wait. It will not hurt him to be bound there and meditate for a time."

Barbados suddenly seemed convinced. He began shouting his commands, and Sanchez echoed them as usual.

Men also ran to get horses and weapons.

"Catch me in a trap, eh?" Barbados cried. "I can arrange a trap myself, and not in the cañon!"

He rushed away, shrieking more orders. Don Audre Ruiz, fastened to the stake, was forgotten for the moment. Fray Felipe approached him.

"It was the only way, *caballero*," the gentle *fray* said. "It would have been far better to have let the traitor wipe out these rogues entirely, but I had to save your life. And the soldiers will triumph when they come. Right is on their side and fights with them. Also Señor Zorro is at liberty!"

"Loose me, fray!"

"I cannot, *señor*. There is one chain that is too strong for me. But they have forgotten you now. I'll search for some tool with which I can remove the chain. The ropes and the leather thongs will be easy."

Fray Felipe bowed his head and shuffled away. Don Audre Ruiz remained lashed to the stake.

TWENTY-EIGHT
UNEXPECTED HELP

LEFT behind helpless in the guard room of the *presidio*, Señor Zorro fought to control his emotions, telling himself that he could think out no proper line of action while his brain was in sad tumult.

His case seemed hopeless. He was unable to make an escape, and Captain Ramón was leading the troopers against the pirates. Señor Zorro began wondering whether his good fortune had deserted him entirely. The *señorita* was in grave peril, and also his friends the *caballeros*, and he could do nothing.

But there was a certain outside influence at work regarding which Señor Zorro knew nothing, an influence caused by his just acts when, as Zorro, he had ridden up and down El Camino Real righting the wrongs inflicted on *frailes* and natives.

The native fisherman had guided him to the vicinity of the pirates' camp before dawn, and then had disappeared. Señor Zorro did not wonder at that, since it was commendable in the native to save his own skin.

The fisherman, however, had continued across the hills to San Diego de Alcála to pay a visit to relatives and friends. There he waited impatiently, anticipating news of a fight at the pirates' camp. And, because he admired uniforms, though they inspired fear in him as well as admiration, he drifted near the *presidio*.

He was in time to behold the arrival of Captain Ramón, and later of Señor Zorro. After a time, he saw Señor Zorro's attempt at escape, and watched the troopers gallop away. And then, by loitering near the *presidio*, he ascertained something of the truth—that Señor Zorro was being held a prisoner in the maniac's shirt and would be dealt with at some future time.

The native wandered around the huts of the village, doing more genuine thinking than ever before in his life. He remembered how Señor Zorro, a long time before, had saved his father. He was a neophyte native, and he remembered, also, how Señor Zorro had fought for the *frailes* when they were being persecuted.

The native fisherman did not have to think long on the subject before arriving at a conclusion. Having done so, he went to the hut of a cousin and begged a bottle of palm wine, potent stuff that could make a man mad.

He took a good drink of the palm wine and slipped away, carrying the bottle. He had a short, sharp knife that he used for the cleaning of fish, and he took this out and inspected it, and then hid it beneath his ragged shirt and in an armpit, fastening it there cleverly with a bit of rag.

Having made these preparations, the native fisherman drank more of the wine and gathered false courage. He spilled some of the liquor on his sorry clothes, so that its well-known odor mingled with that of fish. And then he approached the *presidio* again.

One of the two troopers remaining was sitting before the main door, and the other, supposedly, was in the corridor outside the guard room, where his duty called him. The native fisherman went close to the man before the door and regarded him evilly. He held up the bottle and guzzled more of the palm wine. The trooper looked up and saw him.

"Dog of a savage!" he cried. "Know you not that it is against the laws and the wishes of his excellency for natives to drink the stuff?"

The native blinked his eyes at him. "May the devil take the laws," said he, boldly, "and his excellency also!"

"What words are these?" the soldier cried, getting to his feet.

"Every man who wears a uniform is a rascal and a thief!"

"This to me? A dog of a native speaks so to one of the soldiers of the Governor?"

"If the Governor was here," said the native, "I'd throw this drink in his face! And if you trouble me more, I'll throw it in yours!"

"Ha! In that case—"

"For you dare not put me in the guard room!" the native declared. "I have too many friends."

The trooper exploded and rushed forward. "Low-born dog!" he shrieked. He caught the native and cuffed him, and instead of taking the blows calmly, the native fought back. It was too much!

"Into the guard room you go!" the soldier shouted. "And when the *commandante* returns he probably will order you whipped. And I'll wield the lash! Give me that bottle!"

The trooper took the bottle and sat it down carefully, having noticed that it was half full, then hustled the native inside and along the corridor to the door of the guard room. The other soldier looked up questioningly.

"This dog has been drinking palm wine and making remarks about his excellency!" the first soldier said. "Throw him into the guard house. He is fit company for Señor Zorro!"

The door was opened, the native was hurled inside, and the door was closed and barred again. The two soldiers peered through the small aperture in it. They saw the native pick himself up and look around as though dazed.

"Ha!" one of the troopers cried. "He will wonder what it is all about before morning. That palm wine is dangerous stuff."

"And I took half a bottle of it from the dog before we put him in," the other whispered.

"Let us watch a moment before we sample it."

The native glanced toward the corner where Señor Zorro, in the maniac's shirt, was propped up on a bench. He lurched toward him, bent forward, and peered into his face.

"A white man!" he gasped. "In the guard room the same as me!"

He threw out his chest and strutted around the room, as though a great honor had come to him. The soldiers at the door laughed. The native turned and blinked his eyes at them, mouthed some meaningless phrases, and appeared to be dazed again. Twice he shrieked like a soul in torment. He beat his fists against the wall of the guard room.

"*Sí!* That wine is strong stuff!" one of the soldiers said.

Still they remained watching. But the native, it seemed, was exhausted. He slipped down to the floor, crawled over against the wall, and let his head topple to one side. Twice he nodded, and then he began to snore. The troopers closed the little door of the aperture. The fun was over.

Though he had recognized the native, Señor Zorro had spoken no word. He was not certain whether the man was under the influence of palm wine or shamming. He listened and heard the two soldiers walk down the corridor, then turned his head and glanced at the native again. The native had opened one of his eyes and was watching the door.

"They are drinking your wine," Zorro hissed.

"*Sí, señor!* One moment!"

The native slipped slowly and carefully along the wall until he was within a few feet of Señor Zorro.

"I thought it out, *señor*," he said. "I know those maniac's shirts, for once they bound me and put me in one. And I have a sharp knife—"

"Careful!" Señor Zorro warned. "If you succeed in this I will make you rich for life!"

"I am not doing it for riches, but because you have been kind to my people and to the *frailes*," the native said. "I must do my work swiftly."

He had the knife out now, and began working at the tough leather of the shirt. The thong that drew the shirt about the neck was fastened with a metal clasp, a sort of lock, and so the tough leather had to be cut. The native sawed through it, and loosened the thong.

He stopped to slip noiselessly across to the door and crouch and listen there. He hurried back and began peeling the leather sack off Señor Zorro. He worked frantically, guessing what would be in store for him if he happened to be caught.

"If I escape, then must you do so," Señor Zorro said. "And keep away from San Diego de Alcála for many moons to come."

"I understand, *señor*. And, if I do not escape, remember, please, that I did what a poor man could."

"I'll help you, and I can."

"A good horse belonging to one of these soldiers is just in front of the *presidio, señor*."

"Good!"

"And some daggers are in leather boots near the front door, on the wall."

"Again, good!" Señor Zorro said.

The native slashed the last of the bonds, and Zorro stood and moved his limbs to restore circulation. Then he motioned the native toward the door.

"Stand on that side," Zorro directed. "And shriek as though you were being killed."

The native shrieked. Señor Zorro himself felt shivers run up and down his spine at those blood-curdling shrieks. The two soldiers listened, and then hurried back toward the guard room. They opened the little aperture in the door. They saw neither of their prisoners, but they did see the empty maniac's shirt in one corner of the room.

And then they did what Señor Zorro had judged they would do—unlock and open the door and rush inside. Zorro hurled himself upon the first and floored him, rolled aside just in time to escape the rush of the second, delivered a blow that laid this second on the floor unconscious, got the dagger from the soldier's belt, and whirled to take the rush of the first, now upon his feet again.

"Fly!" he ordered the native. But the fisherman stood just outside the door, waiting to see the outcome.

Señor Zorro had no quarrel with the soldiery, and he did not want to wound a trooper. But it was demanded of him that he make an escape as quickly as possible, and make certain that he could not be followed for some minutes.

And so he rushed his man with the dagger, and the other gave ground and put himself on guard. But suddenly Señor Zorro whirled and rushed backward instead of attacking, darted through the door, slammed it shut, and shot home the bar. Inside were the two soldiers.

"*Señores, adios!*" Zorro said at the aperture. "I regret that you cannot accompany me and see the fighting."

"For this—" one of the imprisoned troopers began.

"Have you ever seen this one?" Señor Zorro asked. And he slammed shut the door of the aperture, laughed loudly, saw that the native fisherman was free, and ran like the wind down the corridor and through the front door and into the sunshine.

A moment later he was in the saddle and galloping like a madman in the wake of Captain Ramón and the troopers.

TWENTY-NINE
THE PLIGHT OF RUIZ

CAPTAIN RAMÓN, riding with the lieutenant at the head of the soldiery, considered his plans.

The captain had told Barbados how to arrange an ambush at the head of the cañon, and he expected to lead the troopers around the ambush and to the rear, cutting the pirates off from their camp, and either exterminating them at once in the cañon or driving them up into the open, where the troopers could ride them down one by one.

Captain Ramón knew, of course and naturally, that the pirates would be watching the advance. But, just at the mouth of the cañon, Captain Ramón could lead the soldiers swiftly to one side and reach the rear before the pirates could understand the maneuver and hasten back to protect themselves.

He had not the slightest doubt regarding the outcome. The troopers were about equal in numbers to the pirates, and while the latter would fight desperately, knowing that capture meant the hangman's rope for them, the troopers were seasoned men who had been through several native uprisings and knew how to handle themselves in battle.

The soldiers had a few pistols, but they were not to be depended on so much as blades and a hand-to-hand conflict. The pirates had a few firearms also, but they lacked ammunition. It would be swords against cutlasses for the greater part, Captain Ramón knew, and the advantage would be with the troopers' swords.

As to his own part, Ramón realized well that Barbados would recognize his treachery at once. And so there would be no protection for him from the pirates after Barbados had passed the word to get him, and Ramón would have to fight with the soldiers as a loyal officer. But he did not doubt the outcome of the combat, and so felt secure.

They rode swiftly and in perfect military formation along the dusty highway, and presently turned off and galloped across rolling country toward the sea. Now they proceeded with caution, flankers out, but they did not slacken speed. It was mid-afternoon, and they wanted to do their work before nightfall.

They approached the mouth of the cañon, and Captain Ramón shaded his eyes and peered ahead, but could see nothing human. The pirates were under cover, he supposed, waiting for the troopers to ride down into the narrow cañon and so into a trap from which they could not escape. Ramón spoke his plans to the lieutenant again, and the junior officer nodded that he understood the arrangements perfectly.

They came to the cañon's end, but swerved suddenly toward the right and galloped along the rim and up a gentle slope, the last before reaching the sea. Captain Ramón expected to hear roars of rage from the cañon, but he did not. He almost chuckled. Barbados evidently supposed that the *commandante* was playing some trick, he took it for granted.

They reached the crest of the slope and pulled up among the trees and looked down upon the pirate camp. A few women and children were running about, but they could see no men.

"Down the slope, then turn and gallop back toward the cañon," Captain Ramón instructed. "Thus we take them in the rear and have the rogues at our mercy!"

"How do you know that they are in the cañon?" the lieutenant asked with quick suspicion.

"Did I not hear this Señor Zorro make his plans?" Captain Ramón demanded with some show of anger. "Am I not your superior officer? They are now in the cañon, expecting us to gallop into the trap they have planned."

"Then they saw us approach," the lieutenant declared.

"*Sí!* And they are wondering what is happening, no doubt. It is possible that they have seen me at the head of the troopers and have noticed that Señor Zorro is not present. But they have not had time to get back to their camp. Their trap has been turned against them. Forward!"

Down the slope swept the troopers, and women and children screeched and ran into the huts and buildings. In a big circle the soldiers from San Diego de Alcála swerved and started back toward the cañon's mouth to hem in their foes.

And, in that instant, the *commandante* found that things were not as he had expected, and that he had been fooled. Reports of firearms came to his ears, bullets whistled among the troopers, and some of them fell from their saddles. And from the huts and buildings of the pirate camp poured the motley crew of Barbados, screeching their battle-cries, eager to wipe out the soldiery that would have tricked and slain them.

Captain Ramón cursed and began shouting commands. The troopers fired their pistols, drew their blades, and prepared for bloody and more intimate work. From behind the largest adobe building dashed a number of mounted pirates, Barbados and Sanchez riding at their head.

"At them!" the *commandante* shrieked wildly. "Forward! No mercy!"

The lieutenant, who was by far the better field officer, was endeavoring to make himself heard above the din. The pirates and the soldiers clashed, fought like maniacs, the troopers at the outset having much the better of it. But Barbados and his mounted pirates joined the battle and fought like fiends, because they saw visions of the hangman's noose if they failed to achieve a victory complete.

Captain Ramón had one close look at the face of Barbados, and heard the pirate chief shriek "Traitor!" at him. Thereafter he managed to keep well in the rear of the fighting, under pretense of handling the men. His blade was the only one not red.

Ramón had no intention of liberating the *caballeros* until the fight was over, for he wanted to claim full credit for rescuing them. He wanted another talk with the Señorita Lolita, too, before her friends approached her. She had not given him the promise that he had expected, and the necessity for it was over, since Zorro was free of the pirate camp. But Ramón hoped to get the promise yet, and have an immediate marriage, saying that he was the one man who could give testimony that would save Señor Zorro if he was tried for conspiracy against the Governor.

The battle waged around him. Barbados and his pirate crew were endeavoring to keep between the troopers and the adobe building wherein the *caballeros* were held prisoners. The *caballeros* were crowding at the little windows, watching the fight. Don Audre Ruiz was still bound to the stake, for Fray Felipe had been unable to reach him before the fighting began, and now the aged *fray* was busy with the wounded men.

The *señorita* was under the close guard of a single pirate appointed to the task by Barbados. She was in one of the buildings, and Captain Ramón did not know where to find her. Convinced of the *commandante's* treachery, Barbados had no thought of letting him get possession of the *señorita*. She could be held for ransom, the pirate chief decided.

Back and forth across the open space, up and down the sandy beach the fight progressed. Here groups of men were battling like fiends, here one pursued a lone enemy. The women and children were keeping to the huts.

"Fire the place!" Captain Ramón was ordering. "Burn them out!"

Some of the troopers were quick to do his bidding. A pistol flash was enough. The poor huts began burning fiercely, the dry palm fronds with which they were manufactured flaming instantly.

Ramón began to worry some. The battle seemed an even thing. Both sides had lost many men, and the two forces now were about even. It came to his mind that, unless the soldiers triumphed very soon, he would have to release the *caballeros* and let them join in the fray.

Back toward the slope the pirates drove the remaining troopers. And there the battle waged at some distance from the burning huts of the pirate camp. The women tried to quench the flames, but could not. The wind from the sea carried flaming pieces of palm frond and fired more huts.

Don Audre Ruiz had tugged at his bonds until almost exhausted, but had been unable to get free. Once the battle surged near him, and then away again. Clouds of smoke from the burning huts rolled over him, surged around him. Great chunks of flaming material floated past him on the still breeze.

Don Audre wondered whether the pirates were to be victorious, whether, in the end, they would roast him at the stake, as they had started to do. He choked in the dense smoke; his eyes smarted and then pained; he tried to see how the fight was going, but could only get a glimpse now and then.

And then he saw something that caused a thrill of horror to pass through him. One of the burning brands had fallen at the edge of the pile of fuel about the stake. It smoldered, burst into flames again. The fuel caught, and the flames spread.

Don Audre Ruiz, helpless against the stake, watched the flames creep nearer, the fire spread and become more raging. Once more he struggled hopelessly against the chain and ropes that held him fast. What irony was this that he should burn without human hands firing the fuel?

Already he could feel the heat of the flames. Slowly they were eating their way toward him through the heaps of fuel the pirates had dropped. Soon they would touch him, smoke and fire would engulf him, and later men would find naught but his charred remains.

THIRTY
FRAY FELIPE GETS HIS GOBLET

SEÑOR ZORRO THANKED his saints that the horse he had seized in front of the *presidio* at San Diego de Alcála was a noble animal of endurance and speed.

He kicked at the mount's flanks and rode like the wind in the wake of the troopers. He knew that he was gaining on them, but they had such an advantage of time that he realized he could not reach the pirate camp before Ramón and his soldiers.

As his horse negotiated the last slope before reaching the sea, Señor Zorro could hear, coming from a distance, the din of battle. He stopped his mount in the fringe of trees and looked down upon the scene.

The soldiers and pirates were fighting hotly at some distance from the buildings. The huts were ablaze. Women and children were trying to escape into the brush. These things Señor Zorro saw at a glance, and also that the fight was an even one, with the advantage to neither force.

He ascertained that the *caballeros* were still prisoners. Only a moment he hesitated, and then he kicked at the horse's flanks again and raced the animal down the slope. The fight was to one side of him, and so he encountered neither soldier nor pirate. He had a glimpse of Ramón in the distance, and believed that Ramón saw him in turn. He rode wildly among the blazing huts, and so came to the adobe building where the prisoners were housed.

Señor Zorro sprang from his horse and dashed into the building. With a metal bar, he broke the lock of the inner door and shrieked to the *caballeros* that they were free.

"Follow me to your weapons!" he shouted. "Fight with the troopers against the pirates! Catch me this renegade and traitor of a Ramón! Remember, Ramón is mine!"

They answered him with glad shouts and rushed at his heels out of the building and toward the hut where the captured weapons had been placed, and before which there were no guards now. The roof of the hut already was blazing.

Señor Zorro kicked open the door, dashed inside, and began tossing out swords. The *caballeros* rushed forward, shouting as they claimed their weapons. Zorro dashed outside again, his own beloved blade in his hand. Already the *caballeros* were running toward the fight.

"Zorro, by the saints!" It was the bellowing voice of Sergeant Gonzales that hailed him. "What is this talk of my captain being a traitor?"

"He is!" Zorro cried. "He was in league with the pirates, and then turned against them. He is a double traitor! Forward, sergeant! Use your blade well! Ruiz! Where is Ruiz?"

"The devils took him out to roast him at the stake," the sergeant replied. "That was long before the fighting began."

"To roast him—" Señor Zorro gasped.

"Let me at a pirate!" the sergeant bellowed, dashing away. "There are scores to settle!"

Señor Zorro, his heart sinking within him, peered around through the smoke. And then hope flamed within him again, for in the distance he saw Don Audre Ruiz, the flames leaping around him. Señor Zorro ran swiftly through the billows of smoke toward the stake.

Don Audre's clothing already was being scorched. He had turned his head away from the smoke and the heat, fighting to the last to keep from drawing deadly flame down into his lungs, and his eyes were closed.

He did not see the swift approach of Señor Zorro, did not guess that rescue was at hand until he heard Zorro's voice.

"Audre!" he cried. "Audre! Speak to me! If the fiends have slain you—"

Don Audre Ruiz opened his eyes and smiled, and Señor Zorro smiled in reply. Then he kicked away the burning fuel and leaped toward his friend.

"You are just in time," Don Audre said. "I had given up hope, Diego, my friend."

"A moment, and I'll have you free!"

He tore away the ropes and leather thongs, and worked frantically at the heavy chain, which was hot to his touch. He was alert and on guard as he worked, but the fight did not approach him. The *caballeros* had joined it, he saw, and the pirates were being cut down, and some taken prisoner.

And finally the heavy chain fell away, and Señor Zorro helped Don Audre a short distance from the stake and thrust a sword into his hand.

"Remember, Ramón belongs to me!" Zorro said. "Let us take him alive!"

Afoot, they dashed across the open space toward the edge of the fight. But they looked in vain for the *commandante*. He was not in his saddle, nor was he dead or wounded and on the ground.

"Find him!" Zorro cried. "He will be trying to get the *señorita* away!"

They ran toward the adobe buildings to commence their frantic search. They watched the slope, and the beach in either direction, half expecting to see the *commandante* carrying Señorita Lolita away on his horse.

"Find him! We must find him!" Zorro screeched. "With me, Audre, my friend! She may be in one of the burning huts—"

And so they rushed through the smoke, calling, searching, fear in their hearts.

Sergeant Gonzales was looking for his captain also. The sergeant told himself that he was in a quandary. His commander and his friend, it appeared, were fighting each other, and the sergeant could not be loyal to both.

He bellowed a challenge and engaged a pirate in combat, took his man, and rushed on. He dodged a charging trooper who almost ran him down, darted around one of the blazing huts, and came upon a scene.

Fray Felipe, attending the wounded, had risen from the ground beside one to find a pirate rushing toward him in flight. The man stumbled and fell headlong, and from the sash he wore about his middle there fell something that flashed and glittered in the sun. Fray Felipe gave a cry and rushed forward. He had seen his beloved sacred goblet!

There was no escape for the pirate. When he regained his feet he found the old *fray* standing before him.

"Beast and fiend!" Fray Felipe said. "Give it me!"

"Ha! Would I not be a fool to do so?" the pirate challenged. "One side, *fray*! One side—or you die!"

The other raised his cutlass to strike. But Fray Felipe could not be driven back by such means while the sacred goblet was in the possession of the other.

"Give it me!" he commanded.

"One side—"

Fray Felipe took a quick step forward and jerked the goblet from the other's hand. The pirate cursed and darted forward again. Fray Felipe caught the descending arm.

Back and forth they struggled, and the *fray* dropped the goblet to the ground again. He was a strong man for his age, but the pirate was young and strong also. He forced Fray Felipe back against the wall of the burning hut, throttled him, raised the cutlass again.

"I warned you, *fray*!" the pirate hissed.

And then he hissed again, a hiss of pain and fright. Through his body a blade had been plunged. He dropped the cutlass, threw wide his arms, shrieked once more, and fell with face toward the ground. And Sergeant Gonzales merely glanced down at him, then picked up the goblet, wiped it against his tunic, and bowed before Fray Felipe.

"Allow me," the sergeant said. "It is a fortunate thing that I was near, *fray*!"

"I thank thee, son!"

"Son?" Gonzales cried. "You call an old sinner like me by such a name?"

"Perhaps you hold more worth than you yourself think," the old *fray* replied.

Sergeant Gonzales could not endure such talk. He grew redder in the face, blew out his cheeks, gulped and cleared his throat.

"I am a rough soldier!" Sergeant Gonzales declared. "And I belong in the battle, which is almost at an end."

"Go, son, and my blessings go with thee!"

Gonzales bowed his head an instant. Then, as though ashamed of himself, he bellowed at nothing at all and charged away through the smoke.

THIRTY-ONE
"MEAL MUSH AND GOAT'S MILK!"

THE APPEARANCE of Señor Zorro at the scene of battle when he was supposed to be behind bars in the *presidio* at San Diego de Alcála terrified Captain Ramón. He had a sudden feeling that the fates were against him—that his treachery was to be punished. And he found that his plans were ruined again.

He had no faith in a personal encounter with Señor Zorro. Something seemed to tell him that such would result fatally for himself. And he had small faith in proving Zorro a traitor after the fight, and a great fear that Zorro and some of the captured pirates would, on the other hand, prove him to be one.

Captain Ramón felt desperate. He had an idea that the *señorita* was under pirate guard in one of the buildings. He would make away with the guard and get her, he decided—ride with her away from the camp and scene of battle.

He could say, afterward, that he had believed the pirates were to be victorious, and that he wanted to rescue the *señorita* while yet there was time. Possibly he could make them believe that he had departed before he saw the *caballeros* released and the tide of battle turned.

He had no definite plans after that. Perhaps, he thought, he could keep the *señorita* a prisoner of his own in some out of the way place, and force her to consent to wed him. Any wandering *fray* could perform the ceremony. Or, all else failing, he could turn criminal, play highwayman, force the *señorita* to do his bidding. In an emergency, a knife thrust in the heart, a secret grave, and Captain Ramón could wander back among men, saying he had seen nothing of her, possibly claiming that a blow on the head during the battle had robbed him of his wits, and that he did not know where he had been or what had happened.

Captain Ramón had a fertile brain when it came to plotting. He watched for his chance, and escaped through the clouds of smoke, urging his horse to its utmost. He galloped around behind the buildings, so that the smoke screened his movements. Behind an adobe building he dismounted, and then crept along the wall toward the front. He crouched beside a window, lifted himself slowly, and peered inside.

There sat the *señorita,* her hands to her face, and lounging near the door was one of the pirates on guard.

The *commandante* drew his blade and crept nearer the door. He waited for a lull in the din of battle and then shouted loudly.

"At you!" he cried. "Die, soldier!"

The subterfuge had immediate results. The pirate opened the door, stepped out a couple of feet, and peered into the smoke. Captain Ramón guessed that the fellow thought the battle was drawing near.

A quick thrust, and the pirate was down, coughing out the blood of his life. Captain Ramón dashed into the building, sheathing his red blade.

The *señorita* sprang to her feet.

"Quick, *señorita*! There is scant time!" he cried. "The pirates are having the best of it—"

"I am safer with them than with you!" she said with scorn.

He reached out and grasped her cruelly by the wrist.

"There is to be no more nonsense!" he exclaimed. "I am master here! You do as I say, *señorita*! Come with me!"

"Beast!" she cried.

"Hard words will not stop me now. Am I to be balked by a bit of womankind?"

He jerked her forward, put an arm around her, half lifted her from the floor, and carried her out of the building and through the billowing smoke. Around the corner he hurried, to his horse. Still holding her by the wrist, he vaulted into the saddle, then pulled her up before him.

"Help!" she cried. "Diego! Zorro!"

"Ha! Call to the fiend, but this time he does not come!" Captain Ramón exclaimed.

But Señor Zorro had heard her shriek. And the smoke lifted, and he and Don Audre Ruiz saw the *commandante* on the horse, the *señorita* held before him. Captain Ramón saw them, too, and kicked frantically at the animal's ribs. The frightened horse plunged away through the smoke.

Señor Zorro was more maniac than sane man as he dashed forward to follow. The fight swerved toward him. He sprang up and grasped a soldier, pulled him out of the saddle, sprang into the saddle himself, and gave chase.

Out of the clouds of smoke he rode, to see the *commandante* and his prisoner a short distance to the left. In the smoke Captain Ramón had lost his bearings for a moment.

Señor Zorro shrieked a challenge, whirled his horse, and took after his foe. Ramón found that he could not get up the slope without meeting Zorro and having a clash with him—the thing he most wanted to avoid. Desperate, he whirled his horse and charged back into the smoke again, thinking to outwit his pursuer.

Suddenly he found himself in the thick of the fighting. Again he whirled his horse. The frightened steed refused to answer rein or pressure of knees, refused to spring forward at the cruel touch of spurs. The smoke swirled away on a breath of breeze. And Captain Ramón found himself inside a ring of *caballeros*, two of whom were holding his horse, another reaching to help the *señorita* down, others reaching up to seize him.

Señor Zorro came to a stop within a few feet of him, and dismounted swiftly, a grim look in his face.

"Down, renegade!" Zorro commanded.

Captain Ramón, in the face of such an emergency, could appear calm, though he was not. He sneered, lifted his brows as though in wonder, and slowly got from the saddle. Once he looked straight at Zorro, and then around the circle.

The fighting was at an end. What pirates had not been slain were captives. Barbados, himself a captive, stood to one side under guard. The lieutenant and his troopers were coming forward.

Ramón called to the officer. "Here is your Señor Zorro!" he shouted. "In some strange manner he has escaped the *presidio*. Seize him and see that he does not escape again!"

The lieutenant gave a quick command, and some of the troopers dismounted and started forward. But they found before them a line of determined *caballeros* with ready swords.

Don Audre Ruiz bowed before the lieutenant and spoke. "*Señor,*" he said, "I dislike exceedingly to interfere with a man in the proper performance of his duty. But I must ask you and your men to stand back for a time. There is a little matter between Señor Zorro and Captain Ramón that must be settled."

"I am in command here, under Captain Ramón," the lieutenant said. "This Señor Zorro is an escaped prisoner."

"Nevertheless, you must remain quiet until the affair is at an end," Don

Audre said. "The *caballeros* are equal in number to your troopers now. If you care to fight it out—"

"Do you realize that you are taking up arms against the Governor?" the lieutenant demanded.

"As to that, we are not alarmed," Don Audre replied. "This Ramón is a renegade and a traitor!"

"Ha! That he is!" cried Barbados. "He joined hands with us, planned for us to raid Reina de Los Angeles and steal the girl. Then he turns against us, plans to trap us! Traitor and dog, he is!"

"And I say so, too," Don Audre declared. "Here are a number of gentlemen whose honors and names are unquestioned, *señor*. If there is a mistake made here this afternoon we will be responsible for it and take the consequences."

The lieutenant looked puzzled. Certainly he did not want to arouse the hostility of those of gentle blood by setting his troopers on the *caballeros*; and he doubted the outcome of the fight if he did that.

"Arrest the fellow!" Ramón thundered. "Are you to be held back by these meddlers?"

An open palm cracked against his cheek as he finished speaking. Señor Zorro stood before him, blade held ready. Don Audre Ruiz took the *señorita* by her arm and led her away.

"Ramón, double traitor and plotter against peace!" Señor Zorro addressed him. "Abductor of women! Foul in word and action and thought! On guard, *señor*!"

Captain Ramón felt like a trapped animal. He saw his sergeant in the ring.

"Gonzales!" he shrieked. "Seize that man! I command it!"

"I do not take commands from traitors!" the sergeant replied.

"I'll have you punished—"

"'Tis you will receive the punishment, when you gather courage enough to lift your blade," Gonzales replied.

Don Audre Ruiz had turned the *señorita* over to Fray Felipe. The old *fray* knew better than to make an attempt to prevent the duel. He belonged to the times, and he understood such things.

"On guard, *señor*!" Zorro warned again. "I do not like to pollute my blade with your blood, yet must it be done! On guard, renegade! Must I cut down a man who will not defend himself?"

Señor Zorro advanced a step. Captain Ramón, his face white, started to raise his sword. He did not believe, could not force himself to believe, that he would be a victor. Yet he could do his best!

The blades touched. And in the next instant Señor Zorro had sprung backward, and a chorus of cries had come from those in the ring.

For Barbados, not watched as carefully as he should have been watched, had taken vengeance himself. He thrust one of his guards aside, snatched a dagger from the belt of another. His arm went up, came forward, the dagger whistled through the air. And it lodged in Captain Ramón's back, the point in his heart.

"That for a traitor!" Barbados cried. "Since I must be hanged, let me settle accounts first! Señor Zorro, you are a man! I, who have fought you, say it! Your blade is too true, *señor*, to be buried in a foul carcass such as that!"

The moonlight came again, touching the sea with glory and showing the trading schooner running up the coast before the breeze. Those of the crew who had been left aboard handled her well, and the *caballeros* gave aid.

Away from the scene of carnage the little ship rushed, the water hissing at her bows. Fray Felipe was polishing his beloved goblet. Don Audre Ruiz and his *caballeros* were dressing their hurts in the cabin. Big Sergeant Gonzales was wandering on the deck.

The sergeant stopped near the rail, leaned against it, looked over the sparkling sea toward the dark line that indicated the land.

Voices came to him, the voices of Zorro and the little *señorita*.

"The sword of Zorro! Let us hope that it has a long rest," the *señorita* said.

"A long rest!" Señor Zorro echoed. "As soon as we are at Reina de Los Angeles we'll be wed by Fray Felipe."

"*Sí!*" she said softly.

"Then years of happiness and peace."

"*Sí!*"

"Yet, I am not sorry for what has happened," said Señor Zorro. "It has brought us closer together. Peril knits hearts, *señorita*."

"Once—when I thought that you were dead—"

Sergeant Gonzales observed a suspicious silence at this juncture. He raised his head and peered through the gloom around the mast. He could see nothing at all save the inky darkness there, but he heard a sound that needed no translation. It was the sound of a kiss.

"Meal mush and goat's milk!" said the sergeant.

www.ingramcontent.com/pod-product-compliance
Ingram Content Group UK Ltd.
Pitfield, Milton Keynes, MK11 3LW, UK
UKHW020654180626
13212UKWH00029B/629

9 798903 000364